SIX RODE HOME

SIX RODE HOME

A Novella
by Michael Dante

Edited by Marshall Terrill

BearManor Media

2018

Six Rode Home

© 2018 Michael Dante

Edited by Marshall Terrill

BearManor Media
P. O. Box 71426
Albany, GA 31708

bearmanormedia.com

Typesetting and layout by John Teehan
Cover Art by Larry Jones.
Cover Design by Mary Jane Dante and Michael Dante.

Published in the USA by BearManor Media

ISBN—978-1-62933-398-4

DEDICATION

★ To all the men and women who have served our country, in all our wars; those who fought, died and survived. The perils and misfortunes of war were no different during and after the Civil War as they are today. I dedicate this book to all; for their service to our country and for their bravery in fighting for our freedom.

★ To my editor, Marshall Terrill, for his constant belief in me and my writing. Marshall is an author with twenty-one credits to his name. I sincerely appreciate his total knowledge of book editing, completing our third work together and Marshall's genuine support of me, my award-winning acting career through the years and as an award- winning author.

★ To Larry Jones, who sketched and painted the original artwork of the six horsemen for the cover of this book. Larry Jones is enjoying much recognition now and is in demand as a western artist. I am truly grateful for his contribution in sharing his talent in his drawings of the six soldiers who rode home.

★ To my wife Mary Jane, for her assistance with this book. Her artistry for the cover design and a commitment to help me make this endeavor a success from beginning to end, was unwavering.

Southern soldiers mustering out

INTRODUCTION

BY MICHAEL DANTE

GENERAL MEAD WAS ONE of the last Confederate Generals to surrender at the end of the Civil War. The plan to join forces with General Lee had failed. He waved the white flag at Montgomery, Alabama, and shortly thereafter, General Lee surrendered at Appomattox. Mixed emotions dominated the vociferous atmosphere amongst the troops that day. Defeat was not easy to accept, but for most of the battle-weary soldiers, the Civil War was finally over and the journey home was uppermost on their minds. Six veteran horse soldiers, who fought hard and played hard, side-by-side, from Shiloh to Montgomery, Alabama, with General Mead, now stood in single file, waited their turn to be discharged and receive their mustering out pay. The line moved very slowly to the sergeant's desk and the last six men looked forward to the long ride home, together. The look on their faces was telling; the war was finally over and now they would be going home. The men all knew the long journey would allow them plenty of time to think of what lay ahead, with doubt and fear of the unknown upon their arrival. They struggled with tremendous difficulty writing, sending and receiving mail. Anxiety had dominated their expectations throughout the journey, for these six men that rode home.

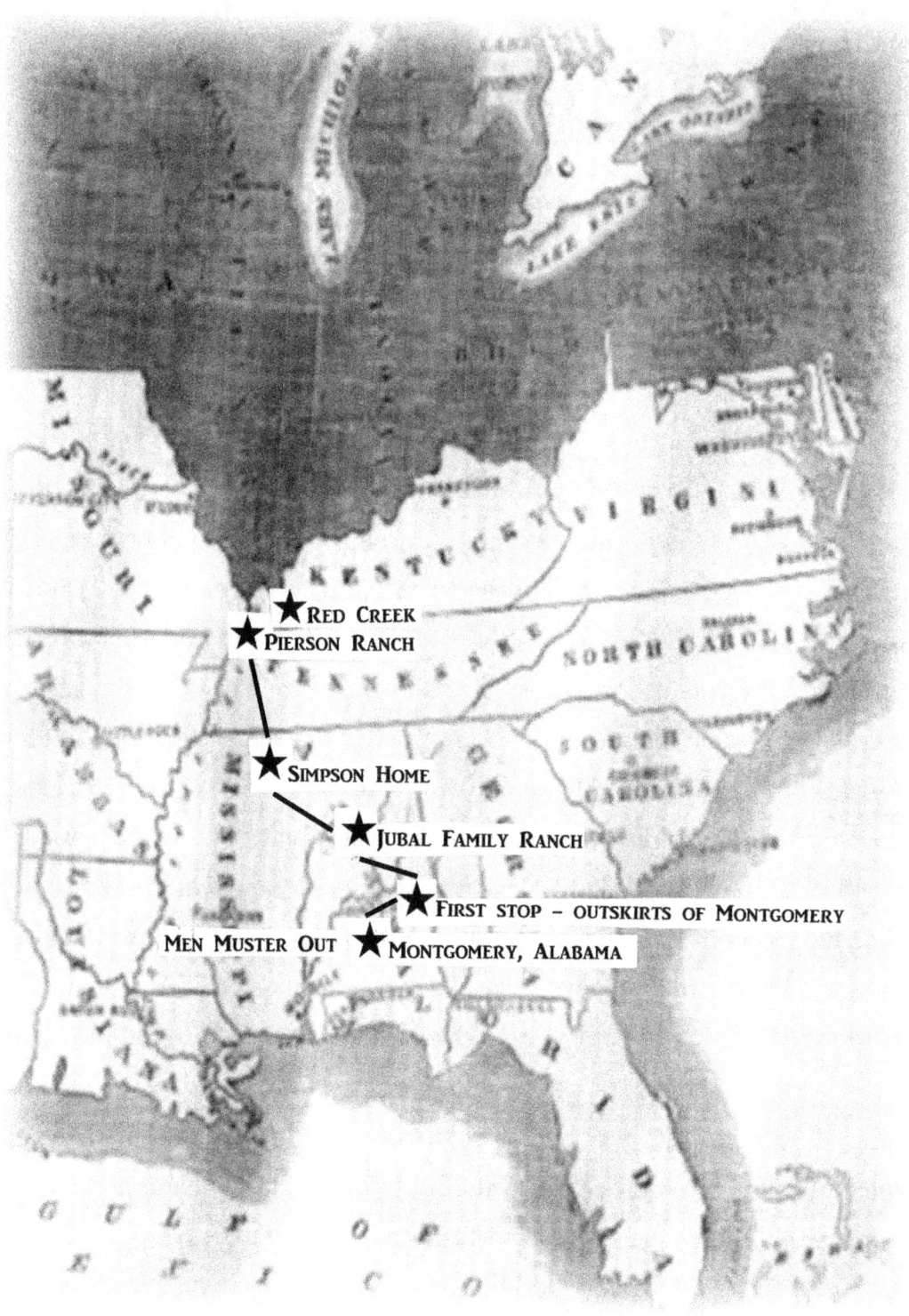

Map of journey

SIX RODE HOME

THE SUN WAS HIGH, very hot and dry. One by one, six riders in rapid succession pulled the reins of their horses up and expertly came to a halt alongside one another at the top of a knoll that overlooked the beautiful open country below, with an inviting town on the other side. Their faces were weary and dust covered that indicated they had traveled long and far.

From left to right sat Cole, physically fit with rugged good looks, the leader of the group. He possessed a quiet strength and intensity about him. Alongside of him was Trotter, the oldest of the group; a tough weather-beaten rebel with an inscrutable and unpredictable manner, who spoke with a gravel voice. Next to him was Cole's younger brother, Pender, a tall handsome, likeable looking character with an infectious sense of humor who always looked for some kind of excitement. On his left was Jubal, a thin, gaunt-faced, reckless young man. On the lineup next to him was Big Black, a muscular black man of a few words, beholden to no one but Cole, who had earned his undying loyalty and friendship. His regular wardrobe was a black shirt, black pants and wide light-colored suspenders. At the end was Simpson, a young, typical farm boy with a sturdy build, slow talking and very sensitive.

3

Trotter stood in his stirrups and addressed all of them, "Alright, you all know what to do." He glanced toward

Cole for approval, "Right, Cole?" Cole pulled his hat down, spurred his horse and rode out first as the others followed in tandem. The six riders headed into town and slowly looked it over as they moved closer to the heart of things. Four of the riders, Trotter, Pender, Jubal and Simpson, reined up in front of the town saloon. The usual early day activities with various inhabitants in this small town were in motion.

Trotter removed a blanket from his bedroll and started for the saloon with Pender, Jubal and Simpson, as Cole and Big Black broke from the group and headed for the general store across the street. Cole, to the others, "We'll get the grub and meet you back here."

Trotter didn't turn his head or break his stride. He simply gestured an okay with his hand, then pushed his way through the swinging entrance doors to the saloon with the other three following him inside. As the four men entered they stopped to survey the room and the noisy crowd, then stepped briskly toward the bar. Pender, Jubal and Simpson relaxed momentarily with their elbows propped against the bar facing the room. Their eyes scanned the gambling activities and then fixed on the waitress-like showgirls moving gracefully around the room. Trotter motioned and called the bartender over, "Give me twelve bottles of the finest whiskey you got in the house."

The bartender's face registered with shock. He mumbled to himself. "Twelve bottles of whiskey?" and continued speaking out loud, "comin' right up." The bartender pulled the whiskey bottles out from under the counter, bringing them to the top of the bar in front of Trotter, who unfolded his blanket and instructed the bartender while tapping it, "Put them all right here."

Saloon in town

As he placed the last of the twelve bottles on the blanket, Trotter collared him and whispered something to him in his ear. The bartender nodded and signaled to one of the very attractive ladies of the house to see him. She worked her way through the crowd toward the bar as Trotter grabbed the ends of the blanket, tied them into a big knot and cradled the twelve bottles of whiskey. He turned his attention toward her as she approached the bar catching Pender's eye, as well.

Pender made a quick move with a broad smile while he removed his hat, "Howdy ma'am. I'm Pender, this here's Jubal, Simpson and that's Trotter." She obliged, "My name is Maggie." Simpson and Jubal nodded, quickly acknowledging the introduction, while Trotter tipped his hat slightly. Maggie, with a knowing look, "Well, you ready?" They were all pleased with her directness and smiled. Pender very impressed, "Ready as ever."

Simpson beamed and Trotter appraised her surreptitiously for a moment. Trotter reached into his shirt pocket and threw some gold coins on the bar to the waiting bartender and pulled his hat down, "Much obliged."

He grabbed the bundle carefully and moved toward the doors to exit as the others followed with Maggie. The bartender watched them leave and shook his head with an inquisitive expression on his face. He watched the four men and Maggie exit the saloon and walked four strong across the street to join Cole and Big Black, who were in the midst of stuffing grub into their saddlebags. Pender promptly stepped forward to make the introductions, "Maggie, this here's my brother Cole and this is Big Black."

Cole touched the brim of his hat and very warmly greeted her, "Howdy, Ma'am." Big Black only nodded tersely and continued to squeeze the last of the grub into his saddlebags and mounted up. Cole, with finality, "We got everything. We're all set. You get everything we need?" Trotter held the twelve bottles of whiskey like a fishing net and lifted it slightly toward Cole. He then turned and looked to Maggie, "I think we hit the jackpot. Let's mount up and get a move on." The four men and Maggie walked across the street to their horses to saddle up. Pender leaned down to extend his arm to Maggie, "Come aboard, Maggie." She grabbed his arm and made a quick leap to the back of his horse. They all rode out until they reached the outskirts of town and approached the flatlands surrounded by trees and a river that could be seen in the background.

When they arrived to the front of the tree line, they dismounted. As soon as Trotter dismounted, he handed the blanket of whiskey by the big knot to Simpson, "Spread the blanket and lay it all out." Cole and Big Black took out the grub from the saddlebags and set it all on the blanket next to the whiskey. Trotter got everybody's attention and threw a steady glance at the men and Maggie, "Remember no drinking 'til the fights' over." He looked to Cole and nodded, stripped to the waist and walked out into the open flat area. Trotter quickly took his shirt off and followed after him. The others ambled over to watch the long-awaited battle. Pender and Maggie trailed a few steps behind the others.

Maggie grabbed Pender's arm and stopped him in his tracks, "Hey, what's going on?" Pender with a quick smile, "Cole and Trotter differed about a lot of things since we've all been together. They promised when the war was over and if they were both still alive, they'd settle their differences before we all celebrated."

Cole gestured with his hand, "This place, does it suit you?" Trotter with exaggerated politeness, "Any place you say." Before anything else was said, Trotter hurled a roundhouse right at Cole, which sent him sprawling. Cole got to his feet and quickly charged Trotter with all of his weight and with a flying tackle brought him down on his back. It was without a doubt a no-holds barred brawl, where everything and anything went, except weapons. Kicking, scratching, punching and hitting each other in the groin, stomach, ribs and face was acceptable. Blood drained from their noses, with multiple scratches everywhere on their faces and even blood dripped from their ears.

Their faces were swollen and bruised, eyes almost shut from the brutal facial blows, but they kept on fighting. The onlookers watched and winced, still rooted for their favorite, yelled ad libs, including Maggie, who was hoping for a quick knockout so they could get started with the party. From the flushed look of excitement about her, there's no doubt these were her kind of men. Tired to the point of complete exhaustion and staggering, Cole and Trotter continued to throw punches even though they were terribly bruised and bloodied. Cole was slightly quicker and connected Trotter with a good combination of punches and then finished him with a straight right to the jaw. Trotter sank slowly to the ground on his back, out cold.

Pender and Big Black lumbered over to Cole and reached out to help him up. Big Black, "Are you alright?" Cole wiped the blood from the side of his mouth with his hand and forearm, "Yeah, I'm okay." Big Black shook his head, "You sure, don't look it." Pender responded happily, "He looks a lot better than Trotter." Jubal and Simpson picked up Trotter and carried him over to the blanket to give him the first swig of whiskey.

He coughed and spit most of it out while unwinding his corkscrewed body to straighten up, "What the hell are you all standing around for?" He picked up his shirt and wiped his bloodied face and smiled, "Let's start celebrating, the war is over!" They all yelled and yahooed while each one grabbed a bottle of whiskey, all except Cole and Big Black. When the others had settled and quieted down a bit, Cole and Big Black reached for the blanket to gather some food and a bottle of whiskey each.

A dark night covered the evening now and they all gathered around the fire pensively reflecting on things in the past and things to come while waiting their turn at Maggie. Suddenly Pender sat up slowly, chuckled as a thought hit him, and then stood up laughing out loud, "You all remembered that early morning at Shiloh when Simpson was taken a crap in the bushes, when we got attacked and he couldn't get his pants on, (laughing hysterically now) as he was running down that hill falling head over heel trying to get his other leg inside his pants? He sure was some sight to see!" His laughter was so infectious, they all joined in. Suddenly, Jubal appeared from the darkness through the trees buttoning his britches and shirt after having just finished his turn with Maggie. Jubal arrived back, with a satisfied smile in his face, "She sure is a lotta woman."

Simpson impatiently, "Who's next?" Trotter said, "How about it, Cole?" He answered casually, "No thanks, I'll wait… go ahead Simpson." Simpson didn't waste any time as he got up as fast as he could, hustled between the trees and disappeared into the darkness. Trotter sat leaning back against his saddle feeling a bit numb by this time, thanks to the whiskey he had consumed. He studied Cole still trying to figure him out, "Cole, you still sore at me?" Cole, shaking his head, "No, I got nothing against you. I'm just not ready yet, but I will be." He took a long slug from the bottle and dropped it. Trotter still probed, "What are you waiting for?" Cole challenged Trotter's gaze, "I'll follow Big Black, is that alright with you?" Trotter nodded his head toward the trees, "That's up to Maggie." He looked to the big guy, baiting him, "That right, Big Black?"

He stared inscrutably at Trotter. Cole broke the contact, "You know I been wondering why you risked your neck to save my life and Big Black's there at Shiloh, and all those other places. We wouldn't be here now if it weren't for you." Big Black listened very intently to the play on words between these two. Trotter almost confessed, "You know… a man ain't worth much without family. The five of you are the only family I've ever known and I'm not going to let anything happen to you, if I can help it." In an unguarded moment, Trotter revealed an intense emotion for his friends and just as quickly, he locked it away again. He lifted the bottle to his lips as Cole and Big Black were both moved by his display of deep emotions and exchanged glances.

Trotter continued, bringing the bottle down from his lips, "Besides, I live to fight, 'cause I like the odds against death. Some people like to drink, like wild women, me, I like war best!" Cole wanted to know more, "Now that the war is over, what are you planning to do?" Trotter shrugged, "I don't know… guess I'd like to get me a spread."

Battle of Shiloh

Cole interested in hearing more, "How much do you think you'll need?" Trotter leaned in, "I know of a bank up north in Red Creek, Northern Bank, if it's still there." He broke into a grin, "Northern money." Cole looked at Big Black, who grinned too. Jubal arrived and the atmosphere around the blanket changed. He was feeling his oats and busting to take on the whole world after his go around with Maggie. Jubal interrupted, "Before you all get too drunk, I wanted to invite you to spend some time at my ranch… meet my folks and kin. It's only a few days directly north of here." He suddenly realized he interrupted something very important that they were talking about. He took a long pull of whiskey to cover his chagrin.

Trotter obliged, "Why not, we're all going in that direction… aren't we Cole?" Cole to Jubal, "Yeah, sure, we'd like to meet your family." Pender's voice can be heard from a short distance away, "Hey Jubal, get your ass back here and finish this card game." Jubal smiled his satisfaction at Cole and nodded affirmatively, "Alright Cole, it's a deal?" Cole nodded, "Yes, you got my word." He took a few steps back and then scooted off to the card game. Simpson entered buttoning his shirt and shook his head, "She's something special." Trotter looked at the two small figurines that Big Black had been tinkering with on the blanket in front of him, for a while now.

Trotter, curiously, "What are those figures?" He answered, "Two Roman soldiers, they were given to me many years ago by Cole's father, Mr. Pierson. He was very interested in the Roman Empire history, especially about the Roman soldiers."

Trotter was a little lost for words, "It's your turn, Big Black." He got up slowly without answering him putting the Roman figurines in his pocket and carried his whiskey bottle as he headed toward the wooded area. Trotter nodded and grinned as Cole lifted his bottle high in return, "To Maggie."

Seated on a blanket near the fire that burned steadily and bright, Maggie watched Big Black approach slowly with unknown thoughts that raced through her mind. She glanced up at him with a look of surprise and curiosity. His dark eyes penetrated hers as he scrunched down close to her and the fire. Big Black, read her, "No Maggie, I'm not their slave." Maggie searched for the right words, "How did you…uh?" He overlapped her, "The army was my only chance, thanks to Mr. Pierson."

His eyes wandered to the fire; he stared at it lost in thought, as the flames flickered across his face. There were only two very expressive dark eyes. Those eyes were now transcended to another period in time belonging to a small, frightened black boy huddled around a fire with several other scrawny black children, shoulder to shoulder to keep warm. All of them were wearing tattered remnants of clothing and without shoes. There was a sound of heavy rain splattered against the tin roof of their ram shackled, squalid hut.

The wind and the heavy rain beat against the front door and mice skittered here and there across the room. In the corner of the room, an emaciated black woman rested on an old, worn out cot, evidently near death. She turned her head feebly toward the door as a hulking figure of a stoop-shouldered black man carried a bucket of soup, pushed through the door wearily. He glanced at the woman on the way to the makeshift table. The children's eager eyes focused hungrily on the bucket as he set it down. They all scampered to it, all but one.

A boy remained near the window looking pensively out toward the expansive lighted mansion of their master up on the hill; a stark contrast to their tin hut. Sadly, he turned his head from the window and stared into the fire, the envy and pain of hunger etched on his face.

The flames flickered and danced in his eyes again and brought him back to the present time. Big Black looked directly into her eyes, "I made up my mind then, I was gonna free myself from all of that one day. Soon after that, I ran away and was lucky to land at the Pierson ranch one night and fell sound asleep on their front porch. I remember they woke me up real early and they were all gathered around me… made sure I was okay. From that day on I became part of the family." Maggie, very touched by his story and full of compassion, slowly began to remove her shirt. Big Black watched for a moment and then rose, "I like you, Maggie. Thank you for listening." He turned and walked away.

Dancing fire

They were still camped on the outskirts of town, just awakened after a long night of fighting and partying. Cole glanced to his left and right quizzically as he sat up, all the others were still asleep nearby. He stood up and shouted,

"Alright, everybody up!" He put his hand to his head, feeling hurt and hungover. The sound of his own voice jolted him. He looked to the others who stirred reluctantly and were all feeling no pain. Cole continued to bark at them, "You'll feel a lot better after a cold dunk in the river." The men groaned and slowly came to life, they yawned, stretched and moaned from the night's activities. Cole sprinted slowly in the direction of the river where Maggie splashed and yelled for the gang to come and join her.

Cole smiled slightly and pointed towards the water, "Maggie's got the right idea… she's already in the river." Suddenly the men were wide awake, and quickly bounced back to life as they stripped along the way in their rush to get to the water. Pender cupped his mouth, "Wahoo! Maggie… Here I come." Jubal close behind tried to grin, "Here I come… balls and all." Simpson added to the humor before he dove in, "Head for the Roundhouse, Maggie, they can't corner you there!" He laughed zanily at his own joke.

Cole, Big Black and Trotter trailed the pack to the water. They were all gingerly frolicking and having one hell of a time, like a bunch of kids. Their gear was all packed and ready to saddle up to leave. One by one, they said their goodbyes to Maggie. They were all very respectful and polite to her. She had been a lot of fun; a good sport and they developed a real fondness for her.

Maggie, near tears, "I… uh…I want to thank all of you for a wonderful time and the money. I never had more fun." She felt a wave of sadness as she watched them mount up and prepare to move out. Pender maneuvered his horse closer to her, leaned down extending his arm and whirled her up onto the back of his horse. Pender to the others, "I'll catch up with you, after I drop Maggie back in town." Cole looked at her for a long moment and wanted to say something, but instead he waved and saluted to Pender. He spurred his horse and rode out with the others.

Pender and Maggie quickly split from the group and rode one way while the others took the road leading from town. Maggie held one arm around Pender's waist and waved with the other until they were lost from view. Cole, Big Black, Trotter, Jubal and Simpson were riding over the open plains, headed for Jubal's ranch.

Pender reined up his horse, brought him to a complete stop and looked in the direction of a small house. There was a posted sign out front reading "Preacher Nathaniel Williams." He spurred his horse and headed directly for it. He dismounted and reached up to help Maggie down. She was puzzled, "Why are we stopping here?" Pender smiled, "Because we're gonna get married here." He lifted her down from the horse. Maggie was shocked, "You're crazy… you know what I am." Pender quickly answered, "I know what you've been, Maggie, and from here on in, you're gonna be my wife." She looked at him strangely. He began to pull her by the hand towards the preacher's house. Pender was not taking 'no' for an answer, "Now come on." Maggie pulled in the opposite direction and made him struggle to keep her moving along with him. She bolted and stopped abruptly, "Now just you wait a minute! I don't know if I can be a wife." He grabbed her by the shoulders, "I've been a gambling man all my life and I'm betting that you can. Now don't argue with me… C'mon!"

He took her by the hand this time and pulled her along faster, but now like a stubborn mule she planted her feet firmly and wouldn't budge another inch. Maggie, seriously, "Pender, quit pulling on me like I was your wife… we're not married yet." Pender stopped and took this to mean she accepted his proposal and very politely, wearing a broad grin, he put out his arm in a very gentlemanly manner, "Ma'am?" Maggie still found all of this hard to believe, "Are you sure you know what you are doing?" She took his arm and tears welled in her eyes. They looked at each other for a long beat and walked peacefully towards the preacher's house.

As they reached the front door, Pender knuckled his hand and firmly knocked on the door. Maggie suddenly pulled her arm away from his, shoved him down and bolted off and ran down the road. Pender was startled and took after her as she ran as fast as she could, "Well, what the… Maggie where are you going? Now come back here." Maggie yelled as loud as she could, "I'm going home!" He took off after her, sprinted as fast as he could and finally caught up to her, "No you ain't!" Just when she was only a stride away, he tackled her and brought her to the ground. They rolled in the dirt and Maggie did a good job fighting him off as she punched, scratched and kicked him. Pender enjoyed her spirit and fire, goaded her on to prolong the struggle, "Whoopee! Ride him cowgirl," laughing now, "You're wilder than I thought."

In the background Preacher Williams exited the house and headed in their direction. Williams confused, "What's going on out here?" He approached the scuffle and leaned down and pulled Pender away from Maggie. Pender, smiled, "Thank you, Preacher, you came just in time… saved my life." Maggie moved to strike him again but Williams stopped her blow. He gently took her hand and brought it down. Maggie was on fire, "He sure did." Williams took charge, "Now hold on you two." Pender rose and brushed the dirt from his clothes, "Preacher, it's no use. I tried to back out of it, but she just insisted we got to get married."

Maggie couldn't believe what she just heard, "He's a liar, Preacher!" Pender quickly grabbed Maggie and lifted her over his shoulder like a sack of flower. He looked at Williams, "She talks too much, Preacher." She kicked, and pummeled his back with her fists, all the way to the front door of the house. As soon as they arrived, the preacher was all business, "I hope you know I'm to be paid before the ceremony begins." Maggie is still flailing her arms away. "Now put me down you… you… I ain't your wife, yet!" Pender, laughed, "I love you too, Maggie. Now pipe down, you're making too much noise." Williams burst through the door with Pender and Maggie almost on top of him. He stepped aside and kicked the door shut with his foot. Williams was all business, "Now that'll be two dollars up front!"

Cole, Big Black, Trotter, Jubal, and Simpson rode to the top of a rounded-off hillside surrounded with a low basin that overlooked a farmhouse. As they dismounted, they heard voices, quickly getting their attention. They moved stealthily on foot until they had a clearer view of the farmhouse, then looked and listened with interest. There were several northern blue coats coming out of the house toting whiskey, food and half dragging a woman. They dumped everything on a makeshift table beside an oak tree to which a man was tied. The man watched helplessly while the soldiers were mistreating the woman. Wild with fury, he strained like a chained beast against the ropes as one of the soldiers continued to molest her.

The soldier had his hands and body all over her, "You wild rebel bitch! I'm gonna calm you down with pleasure." He laughed devilishly and forcibly kissed her. The woman broke her face away from his grip, "Let me go! Take your filthy rotten hands off me! Let me go!" She clawed and swung wildly at him with little effect. He chuckled, enjoying her struggle; the physical contact excited him. He teased her some more while trying to grab and hold her hands. He hungrily and desperately tried to kiss her with his drunken lips. She managed to twist her head away from him momentarily and sank her teeth into the back side of his hand, biting down hard and drawing blood. He pulled his hand away like a wounded animal. The other inebriated soldiers exploded with laughter, each recklessly drinking from their own whiskey bottle. The same soldier moved his fingers slowly over the open wound on his hand and narrowed his eyes with lust.

The woman was petrified as he moved closer to her. He took a step forward and backhanded her across the face with all his strength. She fell to the ground in pain and began to sob. He stood over her and laughed, "I'm gonna tame you yet, bitch!" The woman's husband strained helplessly to get free of the tight ropes that bound him; his face was filled with torment. Another soldier walked up to him and sneered, "What's the matter? Ain't you ever seen anybody playing with your wife before?" He howled drunkenly and took a long pull from the bottle, the excess spilled out over the corner of his mouth and beard. He wiped himself with the back of his hand and moved closer to the man, holding the bottle of whiskey out to him. He still taunted him, "You thirsty?" Unconsciously the man licked his lips. The soldier held a bottle up to his lips for a moment, then lifted it high over the man's head and poured the contents over him and laughed diabolically.

At the top of the hill the five men were looking down and listened. "What do you make of it?" Cole very solemnly, "Looks like an outdoor picnic… took whatever they please." Trotter added his thoughts, "Guess they forgot about the war being over." Cole turned to the others, "We'll move in slowly and quietly. Simpson and Jubal take the left flank, Trotter you take the right flank, Big Black and I'll take the middle. Let's go." The men fanned out and stealthily made their way closer and closer to the farmhouse. Cole whispered to Big Black while he cocked the hammer of his pistol, "I'll take the lover boy."

Big Black nods, "I got the slob by the tree." Cole and the others are now in closer range. The first soldier was still forcing himself on the woman when he spotted Cole and Big Black. He automatically threw the woman aside roughly and went for his gun. The first shot was fired by Cole, hitting him dead center in the chest as the impact turned him around, causing him to fall facedown to the ground. Big Black fired and dropped the other soldier by the trees. The other two soldiers were completely caught by surprise. Trotter, Simpson and Jubal opened fire from both flanks with a loud barrage of gunshots… then silence.

They all moved in quickly, Cole went directly to the woman and gestured to Trotter toward her husband at the tree. Cole helped the woman up, "Are you alright?" She nodded yes through tears and pain, fixed her eyes on Trotter as he untied her husband. As soon he was free he rushed to her. They embraced and she began to sob as he tried to comfort her. Trotter to the husband, "Are there anymore soldiers?" The husband answered weakly, "I'm not sure, but I think there's one more." Cole looked around, "Any of them alive?" Trotter nudged the soldier nearby with his foot, "This guy is stone dead." Simpson, proudly, "Yeah, so is this one." Jubal admired the shot. "This one got it right between the eyes." Cole looked down at the dead soldiers with some remorse. He pointed to a little hillside nearby, "We'll bury them over there." At the riverbank, a lone soldier was crouched down low and drew a bead on Cole through his rifle site. He held his rifle steady and took careful aim.

A loud rifle shot broke the silence that echoed throughout the area. Cole, Trotter, Big Black, Simpson, Jubal, the man and his wife quickly hit the dirt. After a long pause we heard Pender's voice as he shouted from a distance, "All clear." Trotter, bounced up and smiled, "Look here, it's Pender." Pender and Maggie walked briskly toward them, "You ought to know better than to start digging graves before you double check your flanks!" Trotter shook his head, "You sure picked the right time to show up."

They all gathered around Pender and Maggie, obviously happy to see them. Simpson grabbed Maggie and spun her around, "I sure was dreaming a lot about you since you left Maggie." Although Maggie smiled, her eyes betrayed some concern; she glanced at Pender whose face was darkened. Jubal slapped her around the rump heartily, "Yes ma'am Maggie, we sure are happy you came back. Can't wait for you and me to..." Pender quickly moved between them. Cole and Pender exchanged looks. The tension mounted as Pender had drawn his gun on Jubal, "Hold on, that's *my wife* you're talking to." The others all exchanged surprised looks while Maggie stared down at the dirt. Simpson shocked, "Your... what?" Trotter muttered, "Well, I'll be." Jubal still speaking, "I don't believe it!" Pender, firmly, "You better and if I hear one more word of disrespect, I'll blow your head off."

After a long pause, Cole approached Pender with a smile and extended his hand, "Congratulations, brother. I want to wish you and Maggie all the best." The others moved in closer to congratulate them too and broke the tension. Big Black lumbered forward, "Yeah, you got yourself a fine woman, Pender. Good luck to you, Maggie." The others shook his hand and pounded Pender on the back good-naturedly. Trotter was the last to get to them, "Welcome Maggie and congratulations, Pender."

The husband and wife approached the group, both startled from the fear they just experienced while they brushed their clothes from the dirt and dust, "Howdy, my name is Will, Will McGowan. This is my wife Myra." They all turned gently, and acknowledged them.

Cole pointed while introducing the gang, "Trotter, Big Black, Pender, Maggie, Simpson, Jubal and, I'm Cole." Mr. McGowan, sincerely, "It's a pleasure to know men like you." Myra still quite shaky from the ordeal, managed a small but warm smile, "We owe you all a great deal. We'd be proud if you would all stay and share some supper with us." Cole answered and smiled in return as he looked to the others and back to Myra, "Guess we can all use some good home cooked food, thank you." Will and Myra moved hastily to the farm house. Maggie wasted no time and followed after them, "Can I help you, Mrs. McGowan?" Pender glanced after her, appreciatively. Cole and the others began to pick up the dead blue coats for burial.

It was nighttime in the farmhouse and they were all seated at the table, having just finished supper with the exception of a tired and weak Mrs. McGowan. With the aid of Maggie, they poured coffee all around the table, as Myra spoke meekly to the group, "Why do they behave like wild animals?" Cole reached out, "War does strange things to people, ma'am. They were good men at one time, I guess." Trotter jumped in, "There he goes again, apologizing for killing a bunch of crazy blue coats." Cole stopped him, "War's over Trotter, remember?" Trotter disagreed, "You really think it's over?" Cole puzzled, "What do you mean?" Trotter took a sip of his coffee, "I still got a war going on inside my gut and tapped his stomach, tell me how to stop that?" Cole, to the point, "You're lucky no Yankee soldier stopped it for you."

Trotter, bitter, "Four years of putting my life on the line and what do I have to show for it? I got no home, no money, nothing!" A long, tense silence followed. Will McGowan spoke up and changed the atmosphere, "Where you boys headin'?" Cole looked at Jubal, "A horse ranch about a couple days ride from here." Jubal smiled, "Yeah it's directly north, about a two days ride…beautiful country." Cole stood up, "We better get moving."

They all stood up as they collected their hats and gun belts. Cole continued, "Thank you for the wonderful dinner." Big Black took a short bow, "Much obliged to you." Cole made his way out the door, Trotter and the others thanked Will and Myra and said their goodbyes. As they exited the house, each man put on his hat outside the door, a holdover of their military training. They mounted up and rode off. Will and Myra were standing in the doorway as they held each other around the waist and watched them go, knowing these men saved their lives.

The riders had moved across the plains and slowly began precariously up a narrow rocky canyon pass. Cole led the way and when they all finally reached the peak of the hilltop, they brought their horses to a halt and looked down. Everyone was clearly disturbed at what they saw. All of an elaborate well-kept ranch was now in desolate ruins.

Everything was burned to the ground and in what must have been a terrible Holocaust. Nothing stirred. No sign of life anywhere, only mounds of deadly black and gray ashes remained. Jubal was clearly shocked and desperately tried to fight back the tears. They all looked at him with compassion and their looks turned to anger when they focused again on the ruins below. Jubal exploded, "They burned it down. There's nothing left ceptin' the chimney, nothing!" He whipped his horse fiercely and raced towards the gruesome sight. The others looked at each other and quickly followed him down the hillside. Jubal slid from his horse before it came to a halt. He ran frantically through the debris searching, blindly. Finally, he stopped. The fear of what happened dawned on him. Tears were running down his cheeks as he called out, "Ma, Pa, Jeb! His emotions building, "J-A-N-A...!"

As Jana's name echoed throughout, he froze. His face registered in disbelief. He twisted and turned aimlessly, repeating their names over and over. He stumbled onto something and looked down at a charred loom. He stooped to pick it up as a flood of memories hit him,

Jubal's burned family ranch house

as he looked at it. "This can't be all that's left of mother!" The tears flowed uncontrollably. He instinctively wheeled around and raced towards the flower patch on the other side of the ruins clutching the charred memento. He stopped at the site of four graves and four crosses. He was stunned and fell to his knees, weeping uncontrollably and unashamedly, clutching the earth with both hands.

The other men watched and observed in silence, moved by his cries of grief and anguish. They remained silent until Jubal had exhausted all of his emotions. Cole dismounted and went to him. He kneeled alongside of him and placed an arm around his shoulders. Jubal turned to him slowly, his heartache turned into anger through the remaining tears, "You still think the war's over Cole? Would you like to apologize again for those murders?" Cole was at a loss for words and lowered his eyes. Jubal looked at the graves, "Why couldn't it be me? He turned to Cole, "I went to war to keep it from comin' here; from touching my family. They're all dead and I'm alive. Explain that Cole!" He answered him sympathetically, "I'm sorry Jubal, really sorry." There was no way to tell Jubal how sorry he really felt. Cole got up and turned away to leave him with his grief as Maggie quickly approached Jubal to comfort him.

It's dusk and the men have gathered around Trotter, who was scrunched down on one knee drawing his plans in the dirt with a broken branch, "As I recall, the Red Creek Northern Bank's right in the center of town," indicating with the broken branch the center of town. "Sheriff 's office is at the far right," marking the extreme right of the diagram, "and there are three roads leading in and out of town." He indicated where the roadways would be. Pender interrupted him, shifting his feet restlessly as if anxious for some action. Pender, interested, "When do you plan to hit it?" Trotter smiled, "Just after closing, after all those good Northern people have left their money. Then we head south for the Panhandle. The law can't touch us there." After a long pause, Trotter continued, "Well, what'd ya think?" Jubal was the first to accept.

He jumped at the opportunity and answered bitterly, "Sounds good. Count me in." Simpson very honestly, "I made a promise, if I survived the war I'm going home to the woman I love and get married. I'm going to make my ranch bigger and start a family with her," as he shook his head, "No, count me out." Trotter looked to Cole, trying to read him, "Cole?" Cole, positively, "No Trotter, I'm not interested. My father's depending on my help. We have a lot of unfinished work to do and besides, it's a bit too close to home. Red Creek's the closest town to our ranch but I wish you all the best of luck, though." Trotter looked at Pender who was enjoying the romantic physical play, cradling Maggie around her waist and exchanged a glance with Cole. He turned his attention directly at Trotter, "Yeah, we got a lot of work to do. Besides, Maggie and I want to start a family." Trotter looked to Big Black, who turned his attention to Cole, "Am I still part of the family?" Cole moved toward him at arm's length and patted him on the shoulder with a smile, as he walked past him. That said it all.

Cole approached his horse and tied his bedroll behind his saddle and prepared to mount up. Big Black and Simpson tighten the girth of their horses and followed suit. Pender mounted up and folded his arm out to lift Maggie up behind him. Trotter and Jubal stood facing them. Silence took over as they all dreaded saying goodbye. Trotter made one last request, "If any of you change your mind, one week from tomorrow we ride into town to check it out and then hit it the next day." Trotter's eyes betrayed the indifference in his voice. There was no doubt he would like nothing better than for the others to ride with him. He moved to Simpson who was the closest to him and reached out to shake his hand, "Simpson." He moved to Big Black. They shook hands. Trotter nodded, "Big Black." Big Black, with a warm expression in return, "Bye, Trotter." Trotter approached Cole, extending his hand, "Sure you won't change your mind? I'd sure feel a lot better if you were with us." Cole didn't waver, "Sorry, Trotter, all the best."

Trotter and Cole shook hands, "So long Cole, take care, ya hear." The camaraderie between them was unmistakable, despite their differences.

Pender and Maggie had exchanged their farewells to everyone except Trotter and approached him warmly, "Bye, Trotter" they shook hands and Jubal followed him, "Thanks, Cole." They shook hands, as Cole said, "Jubal, if it makes you feel any better, I'm almost sure those Yankees we sent to hell back there were the same ones who killed your family." Jubal paused and mumbled with his head down, "Yea, I pray you're right." Cole, Pender, Maggie, Big Black and Simpson all walked to their horses and mounted up. They turned, and gave one last look at Trotter and Jubal, spurred their horses and rode away. Trotter and Jubal watched them disappear into the distance. Sadness prevailed as they watched the men, who had been like family for the past four years, ride out of their lives.

Cole, Pender, Maggie, Big Black and Simpson rode at a comfortable gate, across the beautiful scenic open country of Tennessee. There was a breathtaking panorama and a feel of the country they just had journeyed across. It was late afternoon and all showed signs of weariness after some days of travel, but continued on. They slowed down considerably, and looked for a good place to camp for the night. They settled at a little plateau near a waterhole surrounded by a wooded area in the background. After they unsaddled their horses, Big Black and Simpson lead the four horses to drink at the waterhole and cooled them down. Cole and Pender gathered up some firewood and some stones to encircle the fire to prepare for something to eat. Maggie spread out a blanket near the fire, a coffee pot, some food and utensils for everyone.

Darkness had settled in quickly and they relaxed around the fire, having enjoyed the needed rest and food. The only conversation that took place before they all fell asleep was about Simpson and his fiancée. He couldn't wait to see her and introduce her to everyone. He expected them to arrive sometime the next afternoon.

The night passed awfully fast and the next morning everyone but Simpson finished their breakfast. From their line of sight, they could see him soaping himself vigorously in the waterhole, singing happily, obviously preoccupied with romantic thoughts of his fiancée. They

Campfire in the woods

all smiled and got a big kick out of his ceremonious preparations. Cole, shook his head, from side to side, "It's amazing what a man will do for a woman."

Big Black with a smile, yelled out loud, "Hey Simpson, come on, let's get goin'. You're gonna scrub that skin right off of your hide!" They all laughed and looked at Simpson, all covered with soap looking like a snowman. He yelled back, "Alright, I'm comin'," as he ducked and disappeared underwater.

The group was already packed and ready to leave when Simpson joined them. He was combed and groomed, and revealed himself to be all spruced up and looked mighty pleased with himself. Cole, appraised him, smiling, "Well, look at that." They all studied the new Simpson with mock seriousness. Pender, seriously, "He sure looks pretty." Simpson became a bit self-conscious, "Awe, c'mon, just wait 'til you meet her, that's all. Just wait." They mounted up and rode out, looking forward to meeting Sally.

It was late afternoon when the group arrived at a flatland location, a perfect area for ranching and farming. Simpson moved hurriedly to the front of the pack and happily looked ahead, "There it is!" They all pulled up and came to a halt on each side of him.

They were all impressed with the first site of a small ranch house, a corral with horses and some livestock. Cole impressed, "Not a bad looking spread." Simpson, anxiously, "Come on, I'd like you all to meet Sally." He spurred his horse and hurried to be with his pretty woman. The others gave him space and slowly made their way towards the ranch house. They dismounted at the water trough near the front side of the house.

Sally came through the front door and stopped on the porch. She looked at Simpson in disbelief. Despite the apron she wore, it was obvious that she was very pregnant. Simpson was in shock and almost inaudible, "Sally?" His eyes continued to scan her swollen figure, the shock turned to hurt. She was staring at Simpson incredulously and subconsciously wiped her hands with the corners of her apron. She couldn't believe he was alive and really there. Sally startled, "Eli?" Simpson almost dragged himself toward her with controlled hurt, "I…I don't understand, I thought you were waiting for me?" A man stepped out of the house and stood behind her, then placed his hand on her shoulder.

Simpson looked at him and then back to Sally dumbfounded, "John?" Simpson was totally confused and the anger was building inside of him. His fists clenched and unclenched. John was just as surprised and shocked to see Simpson as Sally was. They continued to exchange looks of disbelief.

Simpson responded incredulously, "I can't believe it…my best friend!" He lunged at John, landing a haymaker to the side of his head, and then pounced on him bodily as John hit the ground. He began to choke him with terrifying rage, "You knew she was my girl and you took her away from me, anyway. Why did you do it, John, why?" They continued to struggle with each other rolling on the ground. Sally was sobbing hysterically, "Eli, John, Stop it! Please stop it!"

The fight continued but John didn't seem to want to fight. His hands only attempted to loosen Simpson's grip on his neck to try to reason with him. John finally broke away and pleaded, "Eli, please let me explain." Sally cried hysterically and tried desperately to pull

Simpson ranch house

Simpson away, "Eli, I heard you were killed! Don't you understand? I thought you were dead! I wrote to you many times but never got an answer." She began to get through to him. Simpson suddenly stopped and began to listen. Sally, sobbing, "You, never answered me, Eli. You never answered me!" Simpson reacted to her plea and slowly got up and looked directly at her. His anger subsided as the impact of what she just said hit him. His whole body went limp with tears rolling down his face, "Forgive me, Sally I... I never did learn to write."

After several moments of studying Simpson, a new flood of tears broke from her eyes about the injustices of life. Sally took a deep breath, "Oh my God!" John went to her and put his arm around her shoulder. She turned to him and put her head in the crook of his neck sobbing. Simpson deeply hurt, "I'm sorry, John. Please forgive me, please forgive me." He stooped to pick up his hat nearby. Simpson looked back at Sally, lovingly, one last time and then headed toward the trough, where the others hadn't moved since they arrived. They were all shocked and hurt deeply for Simpson. Cole, very gently, "You're welcome to come with us." Simpson was fighting to control his emotions, "No thanks, Cole. I'll need some money to start a new life somewhere else."

He headed for his horse to mount up. Cole watched him closely, "Trotter?" As Simpson rested for a moment in his saddle and glanced back at Cole, "Yeah." He spurred his horse hard and quickly cantered away. They were all lost for words and watched him ride away until he was out of sight. They slowly moved to their horses, climbed up and moved out.

Cole, Pender, Maggie and Big Black had been riding across the wide-open country of Tennessee for a few days now and are only one day's ride from their destination. They stopped to rest before the final stretch to the Pierson Ranch near the Kentucky border. It was dusk and they were all in need of a good night's rest, including the horses. They settled near a row of trees and made themselves comfortable around a flaming orange fire.

Maggie was cuddled beside Pender and rested her head on his shoulder, "Do you think your dad is going to like me?" Pender was caught by surprise, "Of course he will. Besides, he likes pretty women. And you're the prettiest woman I've ever seen." "Thank you, no one in my family ever told me that. I was an only child and my dad was hoping to have a lot of boys to work the farm with him. Mom couldn't have any more children and she died a year after my father passed away. I was only fifteen years old, never finished school, lost the farm and had to take care of myself."

Pender looked into her eyes, "You're never going to have to worry about anyone taking care of you again, I promise you." She kissed him tenderly, "I love you, Pender." Pender quickly responded, "And I love you, Maggie."

Big Black broke his conversation with Cole, "What are you two love birds whispering about?" Cole joined in, "Got some big plans lined up when we get home? And Maggie, you're going to be surrounded by all men, so I know you'll be gettin' a lot of attention." Cole and Big Black expressed a loving smile for both of them.

The night raced by and turned to day quickly. The four of them anxiously rode at a steady pace through the morning and arrived at the Pierson spread in the early afternoon. In the distance they saw the archway, which bore the overhead sign, "Pierson Ranch." They sped up their gate and quickly entered underneath the impressive wood carved archway, then slowed down to observe the activity of all the busy hired hands. They looked with particular scrutiny at several ranch hands wearing blue coats, and then glanced at each other.

Entrance to Pierson Ranch

They stopped in the front of the main house, and were greeted by Sarah, who wiped her wet hands on her half- apron. She was the keeper of the household and the wife of Ben, the old-time foreman. They have been with the family since the boys were children. Ben rushed from the nearby corral to greet them heartily, "Cole, Pender, and Big Black, you look just the same as the day you left." Cole smiled, "Sure is good to see you Ben, Sarah." Big Black warmly looked at Sarah and shook hands with Ben, "How are ya, Ben?" Ben returned the greeting, "Nice to have you back."

Pender proudly joined in, "Ben, Sarah, I want you to meet my wife, Maggie." Ben was beaming, "Well, I'll be darn!" Sarah looked at Maggie in a motherly way. Ben removed his hat clumsily, "It's a pleasure to meet you, Ma'am." He looked to Pender and smiled,

"She sure is pretty, Pen." Ben reached out for Cole's arm, "Come on. Your father will sure be happy to see all of you."

Several other ranch hands greeted Cole and Pender along the way, welcoming them back warmly. The small group approached the elaborate main house with Maggie and Big Black tagging behind. Suddenly Cole and Pender stopped in their tracks. After being gone for four years, they took a look at their father standing in the doorway for the first time. Jess Pierson was a fit handsome man in his late sixties. All of the emotion a father felt, at first sight of his sons returning home from the war was etched on his face. He paused for a moment and stepped out of the doorway, hurrying toward them. Cole and Pender rushed to embrace their father; it was a heartwarming, emotional greeting.

Mr. Pierson, "You look fine boys, a little different, but you haven't changed much." He held Cole and Pender at arms-length and appraised them, "You're not kids anymore. You're both men now and you look good and healthy." Cole returned the compliment. "So, do you, Pa." As the emotional impact sank in, Pierson looked past his two sons. Pender had momentarily forgotten to introduce Maggie. "Oh Pa, I'd like you to meet my wife, Maggie. Maggie, this is my father, Jess." There was a moment of silence, as Pierson gazed at Maggie with an inscrutable look on his face. Maggie hesitated with uncertainty and was anxiously waiting for a look of approval.

Maggie reached out her hand, "Mr. Pierson." Pierson was frozen for a moment. He very deliberately stepped forward ignoring her outstretched hand, enfolding Maggie in his arms. A warm smile filled Pierson's face, "I finally have a daughter and a beautiful one at that." The tension was broken as they all joined in with happy laughter.

Cole suddenly remembered, "Pa, Big Black has been with us through the war... no problems." Pierson extended his hand, "Good to have you back home, Big Black." They shook hands as Big Black responded warmly, "Thank you, Mr. Pierson." Cole's eyes slowly scanned the ranch, "The place has grown quite a bit." He looked back to his father, "How come you hired so many blue coats?" Mr. Pierson patted him on the shoulder, "The war is over, son. We all have to live and work together now." Cole took a moment to consider what his father had just said, "Sorry Pa, I guess you're right."

Mr. Pierson's eyes went to the blue coat ranch hands who loaded three wagons of ropes, shovels, wood posts and other gear. He looked back at Cole and his mood was much lighter, "You're just in time for the roundup, son. Tomorrow at sun-up we'll search the hills for stray mustangs. You, Pen and Deer Foot, will chase the herd toward us, but right now, you, Pen, Maggie and Big Black are going to clean up and have some supper. We've got a lot to talk about boys." He placed an arm around each one of them, as they walked into the house with Maggie and Big Black following close behind.

The sun was just rising along with Cole, Pender, Pierson, Big Black, Ben and the ranch wranglers. They were all busy saddling their horses and getting ready to ride.

Suddenly a lean, wiry Indian rode in hurriedly, jumped from his horse and went directly to Jess Pierson. His movements were swift, graceful and he was appropriately called Deer Foot, a Shawnee brave. He wore moccasins and soft leather trousers. His right trouser leg featured a long beaded, scabbard knife. His eyes were alert and his posture, that of a proud warrior. Cole and Pender reacted with warmth at the sight of him. They immediately moved to greet him and Big Black joined the greeting just a few steps behind. Cole with his hand extended, "Deer Foot, it's been a long time." Pender, "It's good to see you." He smiled and they shook hands heartily. Cole sincerely, "We spoke of you many times since we left." Deer Foot answered proudly, "And I have thought of you, my brothers many times. My heart welcomes the sight of all of you." He and Big Black shook hands robustly.

Pierson broke the atmosphere and got right down to business, "Deer Foot, did you see the mustangs?" Deer Foot answered quickly, "Yes, near Twin Peaks, in the canyon about thirty or forty head." Pierson pondered over his next move, "There's only one waterhole within miles of here. We'll be sure to head them off at the mouth of the canyon, so they have to run toward the waterhole. They'll be awfully thirsty after that run." Cole was still familiar with the area, "Pen, Deer Foot and me will ride the canyon." Pierson turned to Big Black, "Good. Big Black you ride with us to the waterhole. Let's go!" The two groups quickly rode off in opposite directions.

Back at the ranch, Sarah and Maggie were in the kitchen preparing a hearty meal for the men's return. Sarah is pleased to have a woman to talk to and a young one, at that.

She looked at her like a daughter; the daughter she never had. Sarah knew very well that a woman who lived and worked on a ranch is dedicated to her share of the hard work. They talked about marriage and family and the importance of pleasing their men. Sarah said, knowingly, "There's nothing better than a good, home-cooked meal to keep your man happy." She looked at Maggie and winked. Sarah had a fun way about her and was obviously very happy to have Maggie's help. The meal was quite large, it took hours to prepare. Maggie was very helpful and accommodating.

While assisting with baking the pies and enjoying the experience, Maggie asked, lightly, "Sarah, in all the years you and Ben have been married, what's your secret to a long, happy marriage, besides good food and a warm bed?" Sarah looked directly at Maggie, paused, and spoke from her heart, "You must love each other, above all else." Then, smiled and said, "And always let him think it's his idea, any idea!" They both giggled like little girls, enjoying the words of wisdom and each other's company.

Cole, Pen and Deer Foot were riding intensely, each pulling an extra horse along, attached to a rope. They arrived and quickly dismounted at the mouth of the canyon. Deer Foot motioned to Cole and Pender, "Come." They followed him to several huge boulders. He peered between them and pointed at the sleek mustangs grazing lazily and peacefully below. Their eyes all focused on the lead horse, a magnificent black stallion. Cole, amazed, "What a pretty sight." Pender agreed, "That's the most beautiful stallion I've ever seen!" Cole's eyes flicked upward and he quickly placed his hand on Deer Foot's arm to get his attention. He pointed to the opposite side of the canyon where a small band of Cherokee Indians were about to move in on the mustangs. They were diverted by Cole, Pender and Deer Foot's presence and looked down below at them. Cole responded in a friendly way and motioned Deer Foot to him, "Tell them we'll help each other capture the herd and divide everything evenly."

Deer Foot nodded, took a few steps out to the clearing at a vantage point where the Indians could see him and began to translate Cole's message to them. Chief Running Horse and his braves read Deer Foot's message clearly and after a momentary pause, Running Horse smiled and turned to one of his braves to signal his acceptance to Deer Foot. He turned to Cole and the others, "He accepted." Cole quickly responded, "Good, tell them to work their way along the canyon wall on foot. When I give the signal, they should start driving the herd to the waterhole." Deer Foot signaled the message to Running Horse, who signaled three of his braves to proceed on foot along the canyon. Running Horse remained behind with the other braves. Cole, Pender and Deer Foot cautiously inched their way on foot closer to the herd.

Occasionally, Cole looked to check the progress on the other side. Cole to Pender, "You ride on my left flank. Don't let the leader turn the herd and keep 'em running straight ahead." He patted Pender on the back as he exited. Cole and Deer Foot arrived at their destination ready to make their final move as Cole looked over his shoulder and gave the ready signal to his father.

Pierson and his men had just arrived at the mouth of the canyon opposite Running Horse and then looked straight ahead toward Cole. Cole and Deer Foot tightened the girth of their saddles and mounted up, ready to go. Cole whispered, "They looked very calm. I'll get as close as I can and try to rope the black stallion first. Stay in front, on my left. If I miss, bring me the fresh horse." Deer Foot nodded yes and saddled close to Cole, who was poised with his lasso, ready for action. He stealthily moved closer and closer to the black stallion. Running Horse and his braves intensely watched Cole, ready to make their move. Cole edged closer with the mustangs just ahead of him. The black stallion, sensing danger suddenly turned and spotted Cole. He reared up, whinnying fearfully and galloped off, wildly.

Cole took off after him as fast as he could, twirling the lasso. The rest of the frightened herd frantically began running in all directions. Cole was in hot pursuit, eager for the chance to rope the black stallion before he picked up too much speed. Pender began to turn the herd toward the waterhole. The black stallion was on the run ahead of Cole with his sleek black mane flying in the wind, galloped as fast as he could. Cole had a good angle on him and closed the gap between them, little by little. He got as close as he could and extended the toss of the lasso as far as the rope would let him and came up short hitting him on his neck.

The race was on again, with the black stallion fleeing to the head of the pack, racing urgently out of the canyon to open country and freedom. Pender was doing a good job keeping him from veering left. Deer Foot galloped his horse as fast as he would go toward Cole to give him the reins of the fresh horse.

Jess Pierson, Big Black and the wranglers struggled to steer the herd towards the waterhole. Deer Foot handed the reins to Cole and took the inside track as Cole bolted to the outside, neither one faltered or slowed their gait for a moment. Their movements were precise and admirable. The black stallion maintained his lead at the head of the herd. Running Horse and his band kept to the right flank of the stallions with Jess Pierson, Big Black and the others pinched the gap on the left. After several miles, all of the horses began to tire

Wild mustangs

and slow down except Cole and Deer Foot who are now astride of fresh horses. The chances of roping the black beauty was in their favor.

The additional wranglers were on top of the rock ledge above the waterhole, scanning the open country for any sign of the herd. The remaining wranglers waited pensively by the dirt holes they had just dug, to plant the wood posts and secure the ropes around them when the herd entered the area of the waterhole. The strategy was working like clockwork. The black stallion was at the head of the herd and raced slightly ahead of Cole and Deer Foot; they were all headed directly towards the waterhole. Pender's horse galloped on the left flank of the herd and now joined by Jess Pierson, Big Black and the others. The band of Indians did a good job holding their position on the right flank. Cole kept a swift, steady pace along with Deer Foot who trailed very close behind.

The stallion was still majestically leading the herd, but they were all exhausted and needed water. One of the wranglers on the rock ledge was scanning the territory through binoculars and discovered a minuscule cloud of dust off in the distance, gradually growing larger and larger. He brought the binoculars down from his eyes, turned and shouted, "Ben, get ready, they're only a couple of miles away now!" Ben waved his hand and turned to his men, "Alright, you all know what to do. Now everybody, get out of sight." They spread out and each man concealed himself in a ditch, sliding a wood plank in place overhead to protect themselves from the oncoming herd.

A rattlesnake slithered ominously close to one of the ditches as the horses thundered toward the corral rigging. The black stallion continued to lead the exhausted herd across the imaginary borderline of the corral.

Ben, Pierson, Pender and the others began to slow down, as well. The herd's hooves began to thunder over the wooden planks, stomping on the hungry rattlesnake, flattening it like a pancake. Three of the men merged from the ditches and quickly began to set the wood posts firmly in the ground. Cole, Pender, Jess Pierson, Big Black, Deer Foot, and the Indians rode in and dismounted quickly from all directions. They worked feverishly and pulled the ropes as tightly as possible. They threaded them through the three rings on each post and formed a temporary corral. Jess Pierson began supervising.

"Alright, make sure those ropes are good and tight so we can replace them with the connecting posts." He turned and pointed to the wranglers, "Get those shovels and start backfilling those holes right away." Pierson turned to the opposite side where two other wranglers had just arrived,

"Now throw some of those salt bars in there, that'll keep 'em busy." The mustangs dipped their heads in the water, licking the salt bars, drinking, snorting with satisfaction and getting their fill. The work setting up the temporary corral had been completed. All the compliments were in order for a job well done by everyone. Cole went to his father's side and watched the horses with great satisfaction.

Cole smiled with admiration, "What a fine breed." The horses were still drinking, whinnying, and rearing up. Some of them charged over to the ropes and began testing them, by pressing against the ropes with their noses. The wranglers hurriedly moved the wagon alongside the corral rigging and pulled the long posts from the wagon. They rapidly set them up horizontally, in place of the ropes. Jess Pierson, Cole, Pender, Big Black, Deer Foot, and the wranglers were busy in the background putting all the loose materials in the wagon. Big Black lumbered over to them. Cole smiled, "Well, how was it Big Black?" He shook his head appreciatively, "It was perfect, that was one of the prettiest and most exciting sights I've ever seen." Deer Foot cheerfully approached the group, "Your plan worked well, Mr. Pierson." Pierson appreciatively, "Your brothers did a good job." He looked to Pender, "Rope and give each one of them a stallion."

Cole quickly interrupted, "Hold it, Pa." Deer Foot looked disappointingly at Cole, who turned to his father, "Pa, I promised them half of what we captured." Pierson expressed his disbelief, "Half? What do you think I'm running? A charity ranch?" Cole was shocked at his father's attitude. He answered him with respect, "They have as much right to those horses as we do." He raised his voice respectfully, "I gave them my word. A deal is a deal." Pierson took a long thoughtful pause as he studied Cole, his lips pursed slightly, "I've given them enough. I've fed them, given them blankets, permission to use the waterhole and the freedom to hunt on our land." He looked directly into his father's eyes, trying to comprehend, "I gave them my word and we couldn't have done it without them."

Pierson was very persistent, "Pen, give them one horse apiece." Chief Running Horse turned and talked very seriously to his braves. There was a quick exchange between them and the chief responded, "Half." Pierson answered, firmly, "You'll get one horse each and nothing more." Running Horse's face tightened and his eyes turned to steel. Pierson continued, "Pen, take some of the men and see to it each brave gets one of those mustangs." He pointed to the Cherokee braves, "They can choose anyone but that black stallion." Pierson, with half a smile, "After that's taken care of, we'll all celebrate."

Pender nodded and walked away slowly with his head down past the braves toward the wranglers. Pierson walked over to Cole and slapped him on the shoulder energetically and led him out of hearing range from the others. Pierson, warmly, "Don't be unhappy, son. It just isn't practical to give them half. The ranch has become a large operation. I can't afford to be that generous. I can appreciate your sense of fairness, but it's impossible. Take a look around you and see how many men we have working for us. Nothing personal, I'm not trying to cheat them… it's just business."

A disappointed look crossed Cole's face as he began to move away from him. Pierson firmly placed a hand on his arm in a last effort to win him over.

He softened, somewhat, "Look son, I hate putting you in this position, but I wish you'd check with me next time. Please, try to understand. Trust me that I know what I'm doing." Cole turned toward Chief Running Horse and his braves who rode out fast as they could, without their token share of the mustangs and answered, "Do you?" Pierson slowly turned toward Cole, looking more than a little concerned.

All the men who participated in the Mustang roundup and some of their wives were seated or standing around a richly lit fire. They were relaxed now and enjoying the conversation about the day's work with some fine whiskey to sweeten the sound of music in the background. Cole, Pierson, Pender, Maggie, Big Black, Deer Foot were standing holding a drink of whiskey or coffee, milling around and chatting proudly about their accomplishments of the day, when Pierson projected with great satisfaction, "We haven't had a roundup like this since you all left." Cole moved to the table and grabbed a pot of hot coffee, filling his cup. He gestured to Pierson with the coffee pot, who nodded affirmatively and looked proudly to Cole and the others, "It's just the beginning." Cole set the coffee pot back on the table and turned to his father, "How did you get a hold of so much land and livestock?"

Pierson gently eased Cole away from the others who were now making conversation among themselves. He conspiratorially began, "Just after you went to war, many of the ranchers panicked. They wanted to sell their spreads at any price and clear out, so I took advantage of the situation and it worked out just fine. Boastfully, he continued, "I've been asked to run for Mayor of Red Creek and we start campaigning after we break the horses." Cole was astonished,

"Mayor, politics? That's city life. I thought we were going to work the ranch, breed cattle and horses?" Pierson reacted quickly, "It's all done differently now son, everything's changed. I'm planning to spread out in all directions. Ranching is fine, but the power is in politics and banking."

A disappointed Cole responded, "Sounds like you're really bent on being the big man in these parts." Pierson answered, positively, "I aim to be the biggest man in the whole country." Pierson boasted again, gestured with his hand raised high above his head as if reading off of a sign, "Pierson and Sons."

He was pleased with the sound of the legend he envisioned, on many enterprises, and he slapped Cole affectionately on the shoulder, "Yep, I aim to keep right on going." Cole, with a slight frown, listened to his father's preoccupation with power, money and property. There was quite a change in his father. Cole gave him a subtle look of reappraisal, "Where'd you get the money?" Pierson answered, proudly, "Well, I made a few loans and invested in a couple of successful business deals, which paid off real big. It sure feels good to be on the administrative end." Cole took a long pause trying to assimilate all of this. He waited for Cole's reaction and when there was none, he continued with a look of fired-up ambition in his eyes, "Why, with money and power we can do anything we please, there'll be no stopping us." Cole responded, "And then what?"

He answered without hesitation, "Then we'll have everything we'll ever need. You don't sound very enthused son. Why, isn't that what life's all about? Don't we measure a man's worth by what he possesses?" Cole answered him bluntly, "A man isn't free if he's obsessed with power. Isn't that why we went to war?" Pierson returned his point of view, "You think you'd be free right now if we didn't go into war and fight the British for our freedom?" A confused Cole answered, "Yeah, but you..." Pierson interrupted, and took a step ahead of him by making light of it.

"Ah son, I don't want wars, I want to work and build, with you and Pen. Let's not argue." Cole quickly corrected him, "I'm not arguing, Pa. I just wanted to get a few things clear in my mind." Pierson placed an affectionate arm around Cole's shoulder, "We can keep everybody working. Like one big happy family." He continued with a different tone and subject matter, "I'm running against Tom Hathaway. I'll need your help." Ben broke their conversation, brushing by them carrying a broken rifle box for firewood. He dropped splinters of wood into the fire first and then placed the rest of the box in the center of the fire. Cole's eyes went to the lettering on the box with interest, as the flames began to engulf it. It plainly read, "Union Army – U.S. Cavalry Ammunition."

Cole redirected his attention to his father, who had continued talking and was indifferent to Ben's presence and actions, "You don't have to do anything. I'll do all the talking." He checked his pocket watch and continued, "Time to turn in. Good night, son, see you in the morning." Cole's eyes followed him until he disappeared into the darkness and then pensively returned back to the flaming rifle box.

Cole and Big Black were riding hard, towards the temporary corral built for the wild Mustangs, silhouetted against the moonlight in open country.

They arrived at the corral and dismounted quietly, not to attract any attention or awaken anyone. Their eyes were very alert, as they moved closer to the horses. Cole spotted Ben near the horses, having a smoke. When they approached him, he was very surprised but happy to see them. Ben smiled, "Howdy, Cole, Big Black, what are you doing here this time of night? I thought you were finished with these critters."

Cole's eyes quickly checked the surrounding area. "Where is everyone, Ben?" Ben casually answered, "Just a few of us here. They must all be asleep by now." Cole pulled his gun from his holster and pointed it at Ben. "Hate to do this to you, my friend." Cole quickly put his fingers to his lips, "Shhh, don't make a sound." Ben couldn't imagine what came over Cole. He looked at him with shock and disbelief. Ben lifted his hands up toward them, "What are you doing? Does your Pa know about this?" Cole spoke forthrightly, "Half of the herd belongs to our Cherokee friends and we need your help." Ben shrugged, "What do you want me to do?" Cole, quietly, "Each one of us will rope five of 'em together and take 'em to the Cherokee encampment."

He motioned with his gun in the direction of the horses, for Ben to get going. He continued, "Let's get started." Ben took a step and turned to look at Cole, speaking to him warmly. He pointed to the gun, "You don't need that Cole." He answered him with an apology as he put his gun away, "I'm sorry, Ben. I didn't want Pa or anyone to think you voluntarily had a hand in this." The three of them quietly began to round up the mustangs.

At daybreak in the Cherokee camp area Cole, Big Black and Ben led the mustangs into the center of the grounds. Many of the braves, squaws and children interrupted all activities, at the site of their entrance. They gawked curiously and soon fell behind, murmuring among themselves as they examined and admired the mustangs. Chief Running Horse and his daughter, Inola, were standing in front of his lodge, watching them as they approached. Inola's name means 'black fox' in Cherokee and it fits her well. She is a very attractive woman in her mid-twenties, tall and statuesque with shiny, long, black hair. Inola, an excellent horse handler, was frequently at her father's side. She had known Cole, Pender and Big Black as a young girl before they left for the war. She saw them now, for the first time upon their return, through the eyes of an adult.

Running Horse, Inola and braves

Inola

They came to a halt in front of Running Horse and dismounted. Cole gestured with ropes in his hand, "I have come to bring you your share of the horses." Running Horse replied with respect, "You are a man of your word. You are always welcome here." He then signaled to his braves to take the horses. Inola smiled and said warmly, "It's good to see you back safely." Cole answered, "Thank you, Inola. It's been a long time and it's good to be home." Apologetically he added, "I'm sorry, my father did not understand."

Cole extended his hand to Running Horse, shook it and said, "Peace." Running Horse returned the handshake and in turn replied, "Peace." Cole, with a slight but approving smile, tipped his hat to Inola before he, Big Black and Ben rode off. Inola turned to her father, "Father, he is an honorable man. I hope we see more of him." Running Horse knew there was a crackling attraction between them.

Pierson, Maggie and most of the ranch hands were gathered around the corral, waiting for Cole to mount the beautiful black stallion, which Pender and Deer Foot worked very hard to saddle up. He gave them a difficult time; indeed, he was something special. Cole climbed to the top of the fence. He watched the Mustang's behavior very closely and waited patiently.

Cole was confident but cautious, "Alright, Pen, I'm ready." He eased his way on to the restless bronco. The animal quickly began stomping and jerked his head from side to side, trying to free himself of Cole. Cole leaned forward and tried to calm him down in a soothing tone, "Easy, now, whoa, boy, easy now." Pender was ready to hand him the ropes,

"You all set?" He grabbed the ropes and braced himself, "All set, open the gate!" Pierson, Maggie, Big Black, Ben and the others leaned out a little from the fence for a better view, as the stud charged out of the stall. Cole was astride the wild stallion, as he bolted out into the middle of the corral, bucking frantically and stomped high into the air in an attempt to throw its rider.

They all shouted encouraging words for Cole to hang on. Some of the wranglers had gathered on the other side of the fence, waving their arms exuberantly and cheered as loud as they could. One wrangler tossed his hat high hat into the air, in an explosion of appreciation, "Ride 'em, Cole." On the other side of the corral Pierson, Maggie, Big Black and Ben were totally caught up in the action. His father beamed, "Ride that bronc, son!" Big Black joined in, "Hang on, Cole!" Ben smiled from ear to ear. "Never saw one he couldn't break!" The stallion still bucked energetically and snorted angrily, but Cole's body was flexed expertly to stay with him. Pender and Deer Foot admired and enjoyed Cole's adeptness to stay with the horse. Deer Foot waved his arm and yelled as loud as he could, "Eee...aa...aaa!" Pender, yelled out too, "Stay with 'em cowboy!" Cole still handled the critter superbly and began to break him. Pierson and Big Black sat on top of the corral post, when Pierson turned and said proudly to him, "He hasn't forgotten a thing, stayed on him like he was strapped on." Big Black responded with a loud yell, "Eeee-yah!" The animal's moves were less threatening, a little slower and half-hearted now. Instead of tiring, Cole seemed to have come alive with the challenge of the bronc. The black stallion had clearly been mastered by Cole.

A wrangler rode into the arena and expertly lifted Cole off the Mustang and carried him over to the corral fence while another

Cole breaking bronco

wrangler lassoed a different bronc and prepared him for Pender to break in. Cole freed himself from the wrangler's hold as he reached the fence and jumped to the ground. He slapped the side of his britches and brushed himself off, "He sure had a lot of spirit. I want that Black Beauty for myself." Pierson and Big Black leaped down from the fence to congratulate Cole. "You gave him some ride!" Big Black said proudly, and Pierson joined in, beaming, "You haven't lost a thing, son."

The three of them walked over and climbed up to the top of the fence to watch Pender mount and ride the second bronco. All eyes were on Pender as the mustang bolted out into the center of the corral, bucking and furiously trying to throw Pender. In the background, a wrangler was seen making his way toward Pierson and dismounted. They talked for a while and Pierson nodded his head a few times during the conversation. He answered the wrangler, who turned away to ride out. No one heard what they said, but by Pierson's reaction it appeared to be something important as he moved quickly toward Cole, "I'm sorry, I have to leave now. I've got a very important meeting at the bank early in the morning and I have to prepare some paperwork tonight." Cole stopped him before he took another step, "What about the campaign?" Pierson responded, quickly, "I'll meet you at the campaign platform near the general store, around noon time." Cole reluctantly, "You still want me to go?" Pierson was very firm, "I'm counting on it." Cole paused momentarily, "Alright. I'll see you there." Pierson turned and waved goodbye to everyone as he left the corral area.

The cheering of the crowd brought Cole's attention to Pender, who stayed aboard the wild, painted bronco. Cole and Pender took turns breaking the mustangs until they were exhausted and saddle sore. Deer Foot joined in the hard day's work, clinging to the pommel of the mustang with one hand, as it barreled out of the chute into the spacious corral.

He cried out with a wild Indian yell as he moved with the animal gracefully, almost effortlessly and finally brought him under his control. Cole, Pender, the rest of the wranglers and workmen, were still reacting with gusto, hooted, hollered and thoroughly enjoyed the horsemanship of Deer Foot. Cole hurriedly approached Deer Foot as he leaped on top of the rail. Cole now standing on the first rung of the rail, patted Deer Foot on the back, complimented his expert performance. And then added as he settled, "Did the Cherokees start breaking their mustangs yet?" Deer Foot, still catching his breath, "I heard they're going to start breaking them in the morning." Cole answered, "Great ride, Deer Foot" and walked off toward the wrangler ready to ride the next bronc. Throughout the afternoon and until dusk, the wranglers earned their pay, broke the broncs one by one in the two corrals. It was a long, exciting and victorious day at the Pierson Ranch.

Pierson, Cole, Pender, Maggie, Big Black, Ben, and special guest Governor and Mrs. Nathan Thomas, were sitting and enjoying dinner in the midst of a humorous story told by a chuckling, Pierson, "If he only knew the governor and I will run this whole territory someday, he'd turn over in his grave." They all joined him with a hearty laugh except Cole, who took another sip of his drink, to cover up his disapproval. Sarah, with one of the servants, entered the room and carried trays with after dinner drinks for each person and they offered cigars to the men. Pierson stood up and raised his glass, "This is one of the happiest evenings of my life. How fortunate to be able to sit at the same table, like one big, happy family, with my dearest friends, new daughter in-law Maggie, my boys, Big Black and Ben. With a little luck and lot of hard work, Governor Thomas and I will run the whole country. What you're about to see in the very near future is just the beginning." He lifted his glass higher now, toasting, "To all of you." They all raised their glasses enthusiastically to drink to his political future, while Cole raised his glass half-heartedly.

It was very early the next morning when Cole arrived, sitting proudly on the back of the black beauty at the Cherokee encampment. He was met warmly by Chief Running Horse and Inola. Cole said, respectfully, "I've come to help break some of the mustangs." The Chief smiled, "Thank you." Inola nodded as she agreed with her father's acceptance. They walked toward the corral where several of the braves were preparing the broncs.

At the corral, Inola looked at the herd, Cole followed her eyes and asked, "Which one do you like?" She pointed quickly, "That one!" It was a beautiful bay colored filly. Running Horse left and quickly ordered his braves to rope and get the filly ready in the chute. Cole and Inola looked at each other differently now, their eyes dictated an intimate emotional attraction to each other. Cole was there for more reasons than breaking her filly. The braves corralled the spirited horse and struggled to corner and saddle her up in the chute. Cole excused himself to Inola, and climbed onto the top of the rail, carefully mounting the bronc. He addressed the braves and positioned himself firmly in the saddle, as he gripped the ropes with all his strength and focused for a few moments. Then he yelled, "Open the gate!"

The filly bucked, snorted and darted from side-to-side and tried to throw him. Cole absorbed the rearing and jarring bumps and held on for dear life. Running Horse, Inola and the braves cheered and continued to encourage Cole to keep riding her and hang on. The look on Inola's face was one of admiration and joy. The hard ride continued until the filly's strength and energy diminished, as the arduous ride was coming to an end. Two braves, riding their horses, approached the bronc on both sides of Cole as he leaped on the back of one of the brave's horses. The filly kicked her hind quarters in all directions, finding new energy upon her release from Cole.

Cole was quickly brought back to the railing where Running Horse and Inola were waiting. They congratulated and thanked him again for a job well done. Inola would now be able to handle her beautiful mustang. Cole turned to Inola and said, "I must leave now, I have an important meeting in town with my father. Can we meet again, soon, and perhaps ride our horses together?" Inola answered, "Yes, Cole." The look between them conveyed desire.

It was afternoon on a beautiful sunny day in downtown Red Creek at the campaign area. Cole, Pender and Big Black tethered their horses, including Pierson's saddled horse, behind the campaign platform.

Flag of the good state of Tennessee

They meandered up front to wait for his entrance. A large group of townsmen, ladies and some children were milling around a colorfully decorated platform, discussing the mayoral candidates and waited anxiously for their speeches to begin. Pierson, with his best politician's smile, made his way to the platform, and quickly approached Cole, Pender and Big Black. He was accompanied by his campaign manager, John Topper, a round middle-aged man with a florid complexion. Two of Topper's assistants followed closely on their heels. Pierson greeted Cole and Pen proudly, "Cole, Pen, I'd like you to meet my campaign manager, John Topper." To Topper, he said, "These are my sons, Cole, Pender and Big Black, who is part of our family."

Topper shook hands with them and nodded to Big Black. Cole to Pierson, "You look mighty pleased." He answered him, very assuredly, "Our plans are working out just fine."

He climbed the stairs to the platform, stopped with one foot on the first step, and turned to look back at Cole. Pierson, very confidently, "Like I said before, it's just the beginning, son." He skipped up the remaining stairs, followed by Topper and the other two aides. Pierson and his assistants greeted their opponent, Tom Hathaway and his supporters who had already taken their places on the platform.

The crowd gathered closer to watch and listen to the candidates with scrutiny. Topper, Pierson, Tom Hathaway and his aides talked among themselves for a period of time, until Topper stepped forward to address the crowd in his thick southern accent. He addressed the local citizens, "Ladies and gentlemen, I am about to introduce an outstanding citizen of Red Creek, who is more than qualified to run for office in this town or any other town in the United States." Cheers went up from the crowd. Topper smiled victoriously and extended his arms to quiet the people. He continued, "Without any further introduction, I would like to take this opportunity to ask Mr. Jess Pierson to come forward and be heard."

Along with the cheers and applause, jeers could be heard from some of the opposing party as Pierson came up to the edge of the platform. He thanked him and shook his hand before he addressed the crowd. Topper stepped back as Pierson looked into the crowd and smiled congenially. He raised one hand to quiet the people down and began, "Ladies and Gentlemen, Citizens of Red Creek. A lot has happened in the past four years. The town of Red Creek has survived the war, but many of our men and women had given their lives for what they believed in." A rabble-rousing Hathaway supporter shouted above Pierson's words, "Tell us about it, Pierson!" He ignored him and continued, "Some of them have been fortunate to return, like my sons, Cole and Pender. They returned with new ideas, full of change and many of those changes will be good for all of us." Another rabble- rouser interrupted, "You had already changed, Pierson! How did you get rich so quick?" Another one shouted, "Yeah, Pierson, tell us about it!"

Murmurs of dissent erupted from both sides. Pierson's voice rose above their voices, controlled, and unruffled, "Red Creek needed some changes and I aim to build this town up with those changes." Another voice from the crowd snarled, "You built your pile already, tell us all about the money you made during the war?" Pierson steeled himself to go on with bravado, ignoring the last charge, "It'll take a little time and money." On the word money, Pierson was again interrupted, this time by all of Hathaway's supporters, who were sufficiently instigated by the rabble-rousers to challenge everything he had to say.

Disapproval came from the increasingly angry crowd. The same rabble-rouser, angrier now, "What about the money you made selling rifles and ammunition to both the north and south?" Pierson froze for a moment and appeared uncomfortable. His eyes darted around the hostile group and turned to look at Cole and Pender. They both looked at the crowd as they measured the depth of their anger and threats. Another rabble-rouser spoke out, "Yeah, and what about the horses you sold to the Yankees?" Pierson was aware that the crowd was beginning to pay too much attention to what the rabble-rousers were spewing out.

He inhaled deeply and mustered up a renewed attitude of confidence with somewhat of a forced smile, "Ladies and Gentlemen, there is no doubt Mr. Hathaway has planted false rumors about me to convince all of you that he is the better man. I ask you to look closely at the outstanding citizens acting as spokesman for him. Those fine citizens can be found in the saloon a good part of every day and night." The crowd had become somewhat suspicious of Pierson now, and will not be placated so easily.

They turned and talked righteously to each other trying to justify the suspicions that had been aroused among them. Cole and Pender were clearly offended by the accusations hurled at their father and surprised that he was fielding them, rather than becoming outraged by the untruths, if that's what they were. Pierson was determined to finish what he had set out to do that day, handle himself like a veteran politician.

He continued with a bit of a frown on his forehead, "Well, now it seems I'm going to be forced to reveal several things about my opponent here." When he turned to gesture towards Hathaway, the rabble-rousers started throwing objects at him. All the other men on the platform quickly began to scatter hurriedly down the steps and out of harm's way, as fast as they could. Cole and Pender immediately weaved in and out of the body of traffic and made their way to the platform. They took Pierson's arms and lead him down the steps. At the bottom of the stairs, Big Black pushed bodies aside, clearing the way to get to their horses at the rear of the platform. General panic and pandemonium broke loose.

A fight started and it soon built into an unruly free-for-all. The local sheriff, Clem Johnson and his deputies, made their way through the crowd and attempted to part the brawlers, peacefully along the way. Their efforts were futile until the sheriff fired a few warning shots in the air, which brought an immediate hush and standstill to the crowd. He very sternly shouted, as he surveyed the area, "Alright, that's enough. We will have order or some of you will be spending the night in jail."

Bank in town

Cole, Pender, Big Black and Pierson eventually made their way to their horses. They all reacted to the shots in the direction of the crowd as they mounted up and headed for the road leading back to the ranch.

Trotter, Jubal and Simpson entered the town from the opposite end, riding slowly past the dispersing crowd, not knowing what had just taken place. Trotter brought his horse to a stop, "Was that Cole and Big Black riding out of town?" Simpson responded, "It sure looked like them." Trotter shrugged it off, "Maybe I'm seeing things." He turned his attention to the platform and the people with curiosity, until he approached the Red Creek Northern Bank. Jubal and Simpson had split up, each going in different directions. Trotter hitched his horse at the rail in the front of the bank and in a very business-like manner, entered through its inviting doors. He walked up to the teller's cage, with the teller appearing at the window, as he arrived. Trotter greeted him with a big smile, "Howdy." The teller returned the greeting, "Yes sir, what can I do for you?" Trotter got right down to business as he leaned on his elbows into the cage window, "I'd like some information."

Outside of the one and only barbershop in town, Simpson casually leaned against a post. He was scanning his eyes alertly to all that went on around him. A few doors down from where Simpson stood, Jubal postured for a moment and looked into the window of a clothing store. Every so often, he turned his attention toward the bank. They both checked the time and the activities that occurred in, out and around the bank, at that specific time. Their eyes caught Trotter as he exited the bank and pocketed his bank book.

He walked down the old boarded steps to untie his horse at the post, and took a quick look in Jubal and Simpson's direction, then slowly settled in his saddle and rode out. Jubal and Simpson

Meeting place outside of town

smoothly leaped to their horses and left town in opposite directions, not to draw any undue attention. On the outskirts of Red Creek, the three of them rendezvoused and began their ride at a faster and more purposeful pace.

Inside their cabin, the three war veterans were seated around a large wooden table. The room was sparse and devoid of any comforts or warmth. Only a kerosene lamp and the bare essentials for occasional occupancy were evident. Trotter poured some whiskey into his glass; he knew there wouldn't be a problem at all taking this bank. Only one teller, a back door which they'll bolt shut unless they decided to use it. He downed his drink quickly and poured himself another.

He looked to Jubal, "How much time did it all take?" He answered enthusiastically, "The whole thing took exactly seven minutes." Trotter continued, "Add another three-to- five minutes to bag the money, then we'll be on our way to the Panhandle." He smiled broadly with satisfaction. The others laughed and slapped each other on the back, playfully.

They were happy their plan was close to execution and eager for the action. Simpson exploded, "Hot damn!" Jubal raised the whiskey bottle, "I'll drink to that!" Simpson mischievously grabbed the bottle of whiskey out of Jubal's hand and held it above his head, as he poured it into Jubal's mouth. Simpson reacted, pleased with his prank, "Right nice of you, Jubal." Jubal joined in the laughter at the joke on him. Simpson jumped up, "Whoopee! Panhandle here I come!" They continued to laugh and drink heartily.

Pierson, Cole and Big Black were seated around an elaborate Spanish hand-carved table with matching ornate high-back chairs. Sarah removed the remains of dinner and never once looked up as she went about her task quickly and efficiently. She waited on Pierson with great difference and respect and treated Cole and Big Black in-kind. The room was a testimony to Pierson's success and affluence. It was furnished elaborately and fully geared for his utmost comfort. A large, open fireplace crackled with the burning wood in the living room. There was a bit of tension at the table, as Cole spoke candidly, "Pa, those things the rabble-rousers were saying at the campaign area, are any of them true?" Pierson rose from his chair and went to a cigar box on a nearby table and plucked one out of the box.

He lit it and looked very thoughtfully at Cole, "Son, all of my life I worked from sunup to sundown, always had to scramble and tried so hard to make ends meet. He continued, "Then, when you and Pen were old enough to help out, the Army took you." He took a long drag on the cigar and continued with his eyes, pleading for Cole's understanding, "During those four years when you were gone, everything went bad. I just couldn't keep things going. They threatened to take everything I owned." He paced the room and became emotionally caught up in the memory of that period of time. Cole and Big Black watched him very closely. Pierson continued, while leaning over the table, "I couldn't let that happen, I kept thinking about you and Pen. I couldn't let you come back to nothing." Cole was more offended by his admission of avarice than being sympathetic. Cole continued to probe, "Then what they said was true?" His refusal to understand and agree, angered Pierson, whose voice now began to tighten, "Damn few people in this world appreciate honesty in business; to most it is a sign of weakness, an invitation to failure." Cole stared at him in disbelief, "Then you really did all those things?" Pierson let loose with an explosion of wrath and banged his fist, hard, on the table, "Yes, yes dammit! I had to take the only chance I ever had in my life. Everybody was either making money or selling their land and livestock for practically nothing, it was one or the other." He shook his head, "I wasn't about to let them bury me."

He saw the disapproval on Cole's face. He slowly went to him and patted his shoulder affectionately. Pierson calmed down now and cajoled, "I did it for you and your brother, son. We'll have our hands in all kinds of business." Cole didn't react; he just eyed him coldly. Pierson walked around to the other side of the table and leaned on it facing Cole. "We've just taken over the bank. Do you realize what that means, son? We control the money. Every landowner, rancher and businessman around has to come to us. And if and when they can't meet their payments, we'll move in and take over."

Cole rose from his chair and could no longer hold back the anger he had been restraining, "You can't do that Pa!" Pierson frowned,

"Why not? Why can't I?" Cole, angry, "Because it's just not right and I won't let you do it!" Pierson took a long pause and his eyes squinted slightly at Cole. "They would do it to us, son, that's for sure!"

His hand moved nervously to his watch chain and rested there. He delivered his words very hard and flat, "I'll do it with you or without you. I have them exactly where I want them." Cole had heard enough. He went to the hat rack near the door and fixed his hat on very firmly. He turned and answered him with finality as he exited, "I won't be a part of it." Big Black slowly got up from his chair and respectfully nodded to Pierson as he plucked his hat off the hat rack, while making his exit. Pierson's shoulders suddenly sagged as he looked very old and frightened, realized that he may have lost his son. He ran to the door and rushed out desperately, calling out to Cole as they were ready to leave. "Cole!" They turned their horses and rode off, leaving Pierson with a look of hurt and frustration. "Cole!" His eyes began to water.

It was daybreak when Deer Foot rode up to the front of the main house. He dismounted and entered energetically. Pierson was seated at his office desk and conscientiously poured over a stack of papers and placed them aside one at a time after thoroughly checking them over. Deer Foot knuckled a polite knock before he entered, "Morning, Mr. Pierson." He turned and greeted him very warmly, "Morning, Deer Foot." Pierson got up from his chair and filled a cup of coffee from a nearby sideboard and offered it to Deer Foot, "Coffee?" Deer Foot nodded yes and took the cup. He continued, "Everything alright on the range?" Deer Foot took a sip of the hot coffee, "The cattle are fine and couldn't be better." Pierson changed the subject, "Any sign of Running Horse?" Deer Foot took another sip of his coffee, "No, no sign of them, but I did see Cole and Big Black heading toward the temporary corral." Pierson went back to his desk to pick up his coffee cup and sat down. He turned his chair to face him, with a surprised look on his face, "When did you see them?" Deer Foot thought for a moment, "Oh, a few hours ago." Pierson leaned forward, "I'm worried about Cole, Deer Foot. I want you to follow him and report back to me as soon as they settle somewhere." He nodded and downed the rest of his coffee, before leaving.

Dear Foot rode hard and climbed steadily to the top of a ridge. He settled in a high area and began to scan the open country below. He saw three specks in the distance, who gradually came nearer and nearer. When they came close enough, he recognized Cole, Big Black and Ben. They stopped riding, and after talking for a while, Cole and Big Black shook hands with Ben, who then rode off in Deer Foot's direction, going toward the temporary corral.

Cole and Big Black headed in another direction, away from the temporary corral and home. Dear Foot began his descent from the ridge and started to follow their course. After a good distance, Cole and Big Black brought their horses to a halt. A short distance away, a light glowed inside of an isolated cabin.

They spurred their horses in that direction and when they reached the hitching rail, the light in the cabin suddenly went out. A voice from the darkness yelled, "Take one more step and you're both dead." Cole and Big Black froze and looked at each other. Simpson, recognized them and shouted, "Trotter! It's Cole and Big Black!" The light inside came back on, as Cole and Big Black walked toward the front door. It flew open, Trotter smiled leading the way and Jubal hung one step behind. Simpson quickly joined the group and welcomed them with open arms.

Trotter patted Cole on the back, still wearing a big smile, "Cole, why…you're a sneaky son of a gun." He continued, "By the way, was that you and Big Black riding out of Red Creek the other day?"

Cole nodded a 'yes' to him as they all entered the cabin and closed the door behind them. Deer Foot followed Cole and Big Black to the cabin and watched the reception they received upon their arrival. He watched them until they entered the cabin and turned his horse quickly to leave for the Pierson Ranch. Cole, Trotter, Big Black, Jubal and Simpson are all gathered around a diagram of the town of Red Creek, pinned to a wooden table.

Trotter looked directly at Cole and Big Black, "Well, you made it just in time. Tomorrow's the big day. Are you with us?" Cole, clearly, "Only if we hit it at night, and no gunplay, unless it's absolutely necessary." Trotter's eyes went to each of the other men. They all nodded in silent agreement. He looked back to Cole, "Alright, whatever you say." Trotter leaned forward and pointed to the map and the plan. He indicated with his finger to various spots as he talked, "The bank is here. The sheriff 's office is down the street, here. We'll take this road out of town." He paused and pointed a finger to Cole, "Cole, you come with me into the bank. Jubal and Simpson will be posted on each side of the bank. Big Black, make sure you stay out of sight and cover us, if need be. You are too recognizable, I'm sure you understand. We'll cover our faces with these scarfs; they're all the same color. If there aren't any questions, we're all set to go, tomorrow night."

Maggie and Pender were lying in bed, in each other's arms. Pender stared up at the ceiling. Maggie lifted her head to look at him, "What are you thinking about?" Pender answered her, very softly, "About you, me, Dad, Cole and our future." Maggie tapped his chest lightly, "That's an awful lot." She snuggled closer to him. Pender, seriously, "Dad sure worked hard to get where he is today." Maggie, gently probing, "And?" Pender quickly, "Well, he's gonna need a lotta help. I know Cole won't go along with his business plans and politics." Maggie understood more now, "Oh, I see." Pender turned to her and leaned on his elbow, "Maggie, if it's alright with you, I'd like to settle down right here and work with dad." Maggie is bubbling," Oh, Pen, I'm glad you said that. It's not a bad place to start a family." They both turned and locked their eyes at each other for a long moment. Pender broke the silence, "I love you, Maggie."

"And I love you, Pen." He reached and pulled her to him and they kissed each other, long and passionately.

Deer Foot rode in among several busy ranch hands. He waved to them as he entered the Pierson house. Pierson was just getting ready to leave as Deer Foot made his entrance. He looked at him inquiringly, "Did you find him?" Deer Foot, "Yes, with his friends, on the other side of Red Creek." Pierson was pleased, "Good work. Get some rest and then let's meet in Red Creek later. I've got an important meeting at the bank most of the day. After I'm finished at the bank, I've gotta run over to the campaign headquarters. We can meet there and ride out to see Cole afterwards." They exited through the front door and went their separate ways.

It was night time in Red Creek and the townspeople were all gathered around the campaign platform, listening to Tom Hathaway give his final speech. Pierson, Pender, Maggie, Topper and Hathaway's manager were all seated behind Hathaway on the platform. Hathaway, very smugly, "In summing up what I had been saying the past few weeks, I would like to impress upon you again, that I will keep all the promises I made to you, if I am elected." His supporters all gathered closer to the platform, while they yelled and applauded their approval.

On the other side of town, Hathaway's voice droned on, but finally diminished. There was hardly a soul at that end of town, except Cole and Trotter, as they moved inconspicuously toward the Red Creek Northern Bank. Cole and Trotter continued toward the rear of the bank, while Jubal and Simpson fanned out and took their positions strategically, in front. Big Black had taken his position out of sight, between two buildings opposite the bank. The rear of the bank was very dark and deserted. Not a sound could be heard, except Pierson's faint voice coming from the campaign platform. Cole and Trotter walked cautiously toward the rear door, looked around watchfully as they moved along. Jubal and Simpson join them out of the darkness. Jubal whispered, "Everything's all set." Simpson added, "The sacks are lying on the floor beside the hole." Cole whispered, "Good work. Take your positions."

Jubal and Simpson returned to their assigned places, on each side of the bank. Cole and Trotter inched closer to the building as they scrunched down, and began to crawl underneath it and out of sight. Cole and Trotter emerged inside the bank through a hole in the floor, made by Jubal and Simpson. They quickly pulled the dynamite and tools out of a bag.

Back on the darkened street, Pierson's voice can still be heard in the distance. Jubal looked at his pocket watch and turned to check

Downtown Red Creek

on Simpson on the opposite side of the bank. Jubal looked across the street between two buildings to see that all was well with Big Black, who waited patiently. Simpson checked his watch and looked down the street towards the platform. Inside the bank, Trotter was ready to light the fuse. He motioned to Cole towards the front door to remove the crossbar while he lit the fuse. Trotter lit a match to it and they both scampered to the hole swiftly and ducked down below the floor level. The room was lit only by the rapidly burning fuse on its way to the dynamite. The flame finally hit its mark and exploded the door off the safe. Cole and Trotter rose up through the floor amidst a thick cloud of smoke. They rushed to the safe and began stuffing the money into their canvas bags.

At the campaign area, there was total bedlam. People yelled and screamed and scattered in all directions. They had no idea what happened, not knowing where the horrible sound was coming from. Pierson, Hathaway, Topper, Maggie, Pender and Topper's aide were still on the campaign platform. They were in shock and just as confused as everyone else. They gathered and hurried down the platform steps. Deer Foot stood at the bottom of the stairs, ready to assist the Pierson group. They all looked toward the other side of town in the direction of the bank. Simpson was sitting on his horse and waiting in front of the bank, holding the reins of Cole and Trotter's horses, ready for a quick getaway. He glanced anxiously up the street to see a group of men headed by Sheriff Johnson, Pierson, Hathaway and Topper, all rushing along the way. Other citizens had fallen in behind them, brandished their guns and waved angry fists. Cole and Trotter quickly ran out of the bank with a large money bag in each hand. Jubal galloped up to them and without breaking stride, like a pony express rider, hooked his arm around the two bags full of money and rode off. He disappeared into the darkness, down the road that led out of town. Simpson maneuvered the horses towards Trotter and Cole to hand them the reins without losing time.

They jumped quickly on to their horses with their backs toward the approaching townsmen, and made a clean getaway. One of the local citizens, by the name of Thompson, was the closest to them. He pointed and shouted, "There they go, right in front of the bank! Don't let them get away!" Just as they moved out, Trotter's sharp eyes spotted a deputy in the shadows across the street, drawing a bead on Cole's back. He quickly out drew him and dropped him before he could pull the trigger, saving Cole's life.

All hell broke loose. Sheriff Johnson and the townsmen were all in range, and began firing away in rapid succession, as they all scattered for cover. Trotter yelled to Cole and Simpson over the noise of the gunshots, "Come on, we gotta get outta here, now!" They galloped off in the direction of the open road, at the far end of town, riding low and fast.

Some of the townsmen rushed into the bank. Moments later, one bolted out and shouted, "Sheriff, the bank's been robbed, cleaned out. Not a dollar left!" The remainder of the crowd gathered around the sheriff and the fallen deputy. A doctor entered quickly and a grave look came over his face. He shook his head negatively, "He's dead." Pierson, Pender, Maggie and Deer Foot avoided joining the sheriff and the gathered crowd. They had to hang back when the firing began because they were not carrying any weapons. The sheriff turned to address the crowd. "These outlaws are not only wanted for robbery. They are wanted for murder!"

There was dead silence as the impact sunk in. Then an angry outburst of murmurs erupted from them and demanded immediate action. Sheriff Johnson motioned to the two men nearest him, then indicated toward the dead deputy, "Take him inside, men." The doctor picked up his bag and walked through the crowd. The two men carried the body behind him. The sheriff turned to the men, putting his arm up to quiet the crowd down. With authority, he spoke, "Alright men, calm down. Thompson, you were the closest to the outlaws, did you get a good look at any of them?" He answered quickly, "No sir, they all had black scarves covering their faces."

The sheriff projected his voice with authority, "I'll need as many of you, as possible. We're going to ride hard and fast!" He looked around and most of them yelled affirmatively that they were with him. Pierson aggressively moved closer to the sheriff and indicated to include Deer Foot, Topper and Hathaway, "We'll ride with you." The sheriff nodded his appreciation and turned back to the others and scanned his eyes over the crowd once more, "Did anyone get a good look at them?" There was a long silence, when Topper finally broke it, "I'm offering a $100 reward for each one of them, dead or alive." The sheriff got their attention again, "As soon as we round up the posse, we'll ride out."

Pierson quickly turned to Deer Foot, "I want you to ride ahead and pick up their trail. Stay as close as you can, leave us signs of the direction you're headed until we catch up." Deer Foot nodded his understanding and exited. Pender overheard his instructions to Deer Foot, "I'm going with you." Maggie quickly added, "We're going with you."

Pender looked at Pierson and sharply looked back at Maggie, "There might be a lot of shooting. I don't want anything to happen to you." Maggie was not taking no for an answer, "Remember what you promised? Wherever you go, I go." He didn't really want to agree, "Alright, alright."

A look of satisfaction appeared on Pierson's face when he and Pender exchanged glances. He motioned to them, "We better get moving."

The posse assembled quickly around the sheriff. One of the men shouted impatiently, "Alright, sheriff, let's go." A second volunteer yelled out, "What are we waiting for?" The Sheriff moved to mount his horse, "Okay everybody, lets' get a move on." The thundering sound of hoof beats could be heard, as they quickly rode out of town.

Much later that same night, in open country, Cole, Trotter, Big Black, Jubal and Simpson rode along steadily, their lathered horses showed the strain of a long, hard ride. As they approached the riverbed, Cole's raised his arm and signaled to stop. They checked the surrounding area, "This is a good place to rest and clean up." They all quickly got out of their saddles and walked their thirsty horses towards the river's edge to drink as they loosened up the horse's girths.

The night was dark, very dark. There was a distant moon, covered by dark, grey clouds. The wind seemed to whisper an Indian chant, the chant of the dead. A man sat on a horse in the middle of an open field. His arms are out-stretched, facing the blackened sky. He asked the heavens not to take him, although he knew his time was near. The wind spoke to him as he slowly turned around and it was Cole, sitting on his beautiful black stallion, his face and body covered in blood. His eyes were cold as he stared straight ahead. He wanted to stay, but knew it was not to be. It was what the wind told him. One moment he was there; the next, he and his horse were gone, swallowed up by a huge, grey cloud of dust, followed by a dead silence. Inola woke up abruptly from her vision in a cold sweat and near tears. She saw Cole's fate, not knowing what happened in town. She wanted to warn him and hoped and prayed the Great Spirit would give her the chance.

They all kneeled down at the river's edge and splashed their faces with water. Cole spoke up, "We'll walk the horses through the hills up ahead; they need some rest." He pointed upward, "We'll bed down at the top of that knoll for a while, until they're cooled off."

Cole turned to Simpson who had just come up from behind him. He continued, "Simpson, you lag in the rear. Make sure were not followed." Trotter, nodded toward the horses tethered at the trees, "Leave the sacks with us, just in case." Simpson shot him a Military salute and quickly walked over to his horse.

He slipped the two canvas bags off the pommel of his saddle and handed them to Trotter. They secured their saddles and lead their horses on foot to a flatter area a short distance away. Simpson watched them leave and began to check the outlying area, scanning the darkness around him.

It was a beautiful moonlit night, a perfect silhouette of Deer Foot on his horse as he moved across the horizon at a steady gait. His eyes were alert as he peered in the darkness at the ground below. He slowed his horse down and soon brought it to a halt. Like a hunter who has picked up a scent, Deer Foot dismounted and scrunched down to the ground and picked up a handful of earth. He sifted it through his hand thoughtfully and was aware they were fresh hoof prints. Deer Foot rose and went to his saddle to untie something.

He walked over to a thick bush and began to fasten a feedbag to the top of it, as a marker for the posse. When he finished securing the marker, he mounted his horse and continued to follow their trail.

Cole, Trotter, Big Black and Jubal made their way slowly through the rolling hills, walking their horses on foot. Cole led the pack and stopped to point to a rocky area up ahead. "We'll bed down up there." Jubal concerned, "What about Simpson?" Trotter jumped in, "Go fetch him." Jubal answered, "You bet." He doesn't waste any time, as he exited swiftly down the trail. Cole continued to size up the immediate area and pointed again, "We'll pair off and sleep on the ledge between those rocks." He and Trotter unhitched their saddles. Trotter looked at Cole, "How long are we staying here?"

Big Black was busy carrying his saddle to a comfortable flat place, but listened to the exchange between Cole and Trotter along the way. Cole responded, "Just until daybreak, then we're movin' out." He turned to leave when Trotter stopped him, "Cole, what changed your mind about joining up with us?" Cole turned and after a long pause, "Remember what you said a while back? A man ain't worth much without family." He turned and walked away. Trotter stood there and placed his hands on his hips. He still can't figure him out.

It was almost dawn and the posse rode abreast at a steady pace in the open country, as they searched for markers along the way. One of the men spotted Deer Foot's marker. He yelled out, "Sheriff, come here. Quick!" He plucked the feedbag off the bush and quickly headed toward the sheriff. He hastily took the bag from him. Pierson, Pender and Maggie were the first to arrive. They all dismounted and Pierson took the feedbag from the sheriff and examined it closely. The others remained on their horses, but gathered around. He returned it to him, "That's one of my bags. Deer Foot's on their trail. He can't be too far behind them now; by sun up he'll know exactly where they are." Sheriff Johnson held up the marker for the others to see. "Now you all know what to look for. Let's move out!"

They resumed their chase. It was daybreak and Cole, Trotter, Big Black and Simpson were asleep in a patch of rugged terrain. Jubal was positioned between two large boulders, on guard, holding his rifle at the ready. Cole awakened and reached over to nudge Big Black, who stirred reluctantly. He peered over at him, sleepy eyed, then looked around. Cole picked up a small stone and tossed it at Trotter, who instinctively jumped up and grabbed his rifle, in one motion. He looked around, down at the stone and over to Cole, who was determined to get everyone up. "Time, we moved out!" They all awoke, stretched and yawned except Simpson, who was still asleep, a few yards away. Cole nudged him with his boot, "That means you too, Simpson. Let's get going."

He then moved toward the boulders where Jubal was standing guard. From behind he approached him, "See anything?" Jubal did not respond, he stopped behind him, and touched his shoulder, "Did you see anyone?" Jubal's lifeless body fell forward. Cole turned toward the others, calling urgently, "Trotter! Big Black! Simpson!" They all rushed to Cole as he turned Jubal's body over. An Indian knife protruded from his chest. Cole hesitated a moment, then pulled it out and wiped the blood from it across the thigh of his pants. He examined the knife closely, glanced over at Big Black, "Dear Foot." Big Black nodded agreeably as Cole slid the knife into his gun belt. Simpson turned and pointed down below. He urgently called out, "Cole! Trotter! Big Black! Look!"

One by one the posse began to dismount their horses and lead them to the water at the riverbed. Cole quickly reacted, "C'mon, let's get outta here." Simpson looked toward Jubal's body, "What about Jubal?" Trotter and Big Black left to saddle their horses, as Cole reluctantly walked away from Jubal's body. He stopped at the edge of the plateau and stayed back to talk to Simpson, "I'm sorry, but we haven't got time." They took a last, long look at Jubal and quickly ran to catch up with the others, who already maneuvered their horses to journey down the rocky slope. The Sheriff, Pierson, Pender, Maggie, and the posse were all assembling at the riverbed and listened intently to Deer Foot, who addressed Pierson.

"Cole, Big Black and two others are holed up. He pointed in the direction of the rocks, "There, near the top." Pierson was clearly stunned, "Cole?" Pender and Maggie were both in shock after what they had just heard. Pierson moved closer to Deer Foot and grabbed him by the shoulders, his eyes beseeching him, hoping he heard wrong. "You're sure Cole was with them?" Deer Foot nodded, somberly. Pierson's eyes flicked over to the Sheriff, "I can't believe it." He looked back to Deer Foot and mumbled to himself, "I can't believe it. Why? Why?"

Clearly bewildered and overwhelmed with anguish, Pierson's arms dropped heavily from Deer Foot's shoulders. He turned away slowly, trying desperately to understand.

Sheriff Johnson moved closer to Deer Foot and asked, "How close did you get?" Deer Foot answered stoically, "There were five, now there are four." The Sheriff bent down to pick up a stick and began drawing a diagram in the dirt. "Alright men, this is what we're going to do." They all gathered around closer to see, as he continued, "Riggs, you take about six men and encircle them from the left side."

He drew another line on the right side and looked at Thompson, "Thompson, you take about six or seven men and circle around from the right. The rest of you ride with me." Thompson had one final question, "Do you want us to join you on the other side?" Sheriff quickly responded, "No, keep your distance and don't join us in the middle until I tell you. I want to keep driving them straight ahead, so they're forced to keep their backs to us at all times." The men murmured their approval of the plan and returned to their horses. Pierson desperately approached the Sheriff and placed a hand on his arm, "My boy, he's riding the black stallion. Please be careful!" He shouted a frantic plea to the deputies, "I'll pay you all double to bring him in unharmed." A long silence followed as they looked at one another, not sure how to respond. Sheriff Johnson did it for them, "I'm truly sorry about Cole, Jess, but my deputy was gunned down." He paused and continued, "You can't expect us to be too careful with a bunch of killers."

He faced his men, "Mount up." Pierson, defeated, turned sadly toward Pender and Maggie. Tears welled in their eyes as the three of them huddled together and embraced in silence. Deer Foot watched intently, with a heartfelt look.

The posse split up into three groups at the foot of the rocky terrain. Two groups began to encircle the area, one on each side.

The main group led by Pierson, Deer Foot, Hathaway and Sheriff Johnson, moved directly into the hills. On the opposite side of the terrain, Cole, Trotter, Big Black and Simpson were on foot, leading their horses and moved as fast as they could while continuing their descent down the rugged area. Pierson, Sherriff, Deer Foot and the others in the main group were some distance behind, but were slowly closing the gap between them. The posse on the left and the right began to narrow the circle. Cole, Trotter, Big Black and Simpson were now sitting atop their horses. Cole pointed, "We'll head straight towards that steep incline over there."

Pierson, Sheriff, Deer Foot, Hathaway and their group had taken their positions with their pistols and rifles drawn except Pierson, Pender, Maggie and Deer Foot. The posse on both sides exchanged a barrage of crossfire, as the horses diminished amidst the gun smoke and dust. It was the first site of Cole and the others. The Sherriff's plan showed signs of working very effectively and chased them back up the steep incline.

Two of the posse members were winged by gunshots and fell from their horses during the exchange. Only a short distance up the slope Simpson was shot in the back. He toppled sideways off of his horse and rolled down to the bottom of the slope. The others turned and saw him fall, but advanced.

Pierson, Pender, Maggie, Sheriff, Deer Foot, Hathaway and the others shortly pulled up beside Simpson's body. Only Pierson,

Pender and Deer Foot dismounted. Pender leaned down to examine him, and sadly pronounced, "He's dead."

Pierson breathed a sigh of relief it wasn't Cole. The sheriff broke the tension, "Let's go, we'll pick him up later." They rode up the slope to join the others and waited for them near the top. The Sheriff and the group arrived in the center position, just as he planned. They had closed the circle considerably and soon made the final decision for the three groups to move in. They all looked around for signs of the bank robbers at the edge of the incline.

With no one in sight, they stepped back from the edge and looked at each other quizzically. Sheriff spoke out, "They're down there somewhere." Pierson, concerned, "What are you going to do?" Sheriff, "I don't know yet." Pierson answered, "Then I'd like to ask you a favor, Jim. Don't decide until Deer Foot has had a chance to contact Cole. If anyone can convince him to give himself up, he can." Sheriff pondered Pierson's request for a few moments, paced and approached him closer, "What's the plan sheriff ?" He scratched his head for a second and then looked at Pierson. "Alright, Deer Foot can try to bring Cole and the others out." Pierson and Deer Foot exchanged grateful glances.

He went to his horse and took a rifle from his saddlebag, while the sheriff addressed four men in the posse as they stood close by. He nodded towards Deer Foot, "He's gonna need some cover. Thompson, Ellis, stay on Deer Foot's right flank. Riggs and Gregory, stay on his left. There's no tellin' what they might do if they get to him first." Shots rang out from some of the other posse at the top of the slope. The Sheriff and his men ran toward them, staying low with their guns drawn. As they approached, Hathaway pointed, "Just saw 'em move further back into the hills."

Cole and the others fired back at them and revealed their position. Only the sound of gunshots was heard echoing in the hills. Sheriff

Johnson, gestured to his posse, "Now you know their position. It's a good time to start moving in and we'll keep 'em busy from here. Good luck."

Deer Foot quickly lead the way out with the four men following after him, snaking his way stealthily from one rock to another, getting closer to Cole and the others without any trouble. Thompson and Ellis moved a little slower on

Deer Foot's right as Riggs and Gregory kept up with him on the left. From the slope, the posse continued to fire at the outlaws, at will. Cole and Big Black watched as Deer Foot came toward them. Big Black reached down and picked up a good-sized rock. Deer Foot was headed through an open, unprotected area and quickly stepped behind a boulder, as a precaution. He suspiciously examined the territory around him and then slowly eased himself onto the ground and hurriedly began snaking his way over the exposed space below him.

When he got closer to them, Big Black hurled the rock to deter Deer Foot from getting any further. The continuous gunfire muffled any sound as it hit the dirt. Deer Foot was oblivious to it as he continued across the open area and moved more cautiously now. He stopped to look around when a mound of dirt began to jiggle and loosen, finally breaking open as Trotter emerged from underground, behind Deer Foot. Staying low on one knee, Trotter drew his gun quietly and aimed at Deer Foot's back. Deer Foot sensed his presence and was about to turn around with his rifle ready when Trotter snapped, "Stay right there, Indian, where everyone can see you and don't move." The posse held their fire for fear of hitting Deer Foot. Trotter was concealed from their view. He inched closer, "An old Indian trick, and you fell for it."

Trotter's eyes were cold and deadly. Trotter continued, "You ain't gonna follow anybody any more, Indian. Look right into my eyes." Deer Foot stared at Trotter unflinching and unafraid. Without warning, Trotter blasted away, point blank at Deer Foot. His body jolted backward, twisted around and then fell dead. Taking no chances Trotter looked around and crouched low. With his first step forward, he was caught in heavy crossfire from Thompson, Ellis, Riggs and Gregory. Riddled with gunshots, his body lurked forward, twisted and fell next to Deer Foot, dead. A new barrage of gunfire shattered the momentary silence as Cole and Big Black mercilessly fired away at the four posse members, killing all of them, instantly.

At the top of the incline, the rest of the men began to fire rapidly at Cole and Big Black, as the Sheriff hollered, "Let's go!" He gestured with his arm and they closed in on the two remaining outlaws. Still somewhat sheltered behind the rocky terrain, Cole and Big Black looked down at the bodies of Trotter and Deer Foot for a long, thoughtful moment and realized their chances of escape were slim. They exchanged apprehensive looks and reloaded their guns. Big Black glanced toward the slope and saw the advancing posse. "They're coming in all three directions."

Big Black looked at Cole, "I unbridled the horses and freed them." Cole glanced in the direction of the horses, as they made their way down the slope. Big Black continued, "What do we do now?" Cole nodded toward Big Black's gun, "How many rounds do you have left?" He checked his gun belt, "None left." And then motioned to his gun with a few left, "That's it." Cole, "Don't shoot unless you have a clear shot."

Pierson, Pender, Maggie and Sheriff arrived within talking range of Cole and Big Black. The posse behind them spread out. Pierson to Sheriff, "Jim, before there's any more bloodshed, let me talk to them please." The Sheriff looked at Pierson and whipped off his hat and slapped it on the side of his britches in frustration. He takes a deep breath and with finality, "This is the last time, Jess."

Last holdout area for Cole and Big Black

He turned to his men and yelled out loud and clear, "Men, this is Sheriff Johnson. Hold your fire." Pierson stepped into the clearing and called out, "Cole, do you hear me, son? Do you hear me?" Cole pondered his reply, "Yes, I hear you." Pierson stepped further out into the open, close to the bodies of Trotter and Deer Foot. Pierson, "Give yourself up. I'll see to it they go easy on you." All the hostility that Cole felt for his father was evident now. Cole, "You've become everything else in this part of the country. Now you've become the law." Pierson was visibly shaken by Cole's apparent antipathy toward him and hesitated to grope for the right words.

Pierson pleaded, "I didn't realize how much you resented me. Why? Why?" Cole, "Because everything I went to war to fight against, you've become." Pierson was bewildered. He truly didn't understand his son. Pierson, "Everything I did, I did for you."

A disappointed grimace came across his face and he shook his head, negatively. Cole, "I'm sorry we didn't agree on all the plans you made for me." In his desperation to say the right thing, Pierson said precisely the wrong thing. "Give yourself up and we'll work something out." His voice rose, "I'll see to it." Cole closed his eyes for a moment. He tried to shut him out and swallowed harder now, the mixed emotions and pain now building up inside of him. When he opened his eyes, the resentment was even more apparent. He couldn't hold back his feelings toward his father any longer. Big Black listened and watched the exchange between Pierson and Cole, with heartbroken feelings for both of them.

Finally, Cole answered, "It's too late for that, Pa." The blood drained from Pierson's face as he stood in a state of shock that his son chose to die rather than to be with him. Sheriff addressed the posse, "Alright men, let 'em have it." They began firing and moved progressively closer to Cole and Big Black. Pierson stood paralyzed with grief; a pathetic, defeated figure, impervious to the explosion of gunshots around him. Pender, in a crouched position, ran swiftly, darting cautiously among the rocks toward Cole and Big Black, avoiding the crossfire. Putting their backs against a flat boulder with gunshots flying past them, both men were perspiring heavily.

Cole checked the magazine of his gun and there was only one bullet left. He looked at Big Black, who nodded toward his gun. He flipped it open, revealing three live cartridges. Big Black turned and fired two more rounds at the posse. He then turned to Cole and they stared at each other momentarily. A silent, mutual understanding and respect for each other was reflected in their look. Maggie frantically ran toward the Sheriff and grabbed him, and spun him around,

"Stop, stop, Pen went after them." She pointed to Cole and Big Black, "He's trying to bring them out!" Sheriff, "Hold your fire, men!" Cole spoke softly, "You're like a brother, Big Black." Reading him, "You're a good man, Cole." The Romans, when in battle, and overcome by the enemy, chose to fall at the hands of each other.

Big Black continued, "Before we went to war, your Pa told me about the Roman soldiers and he gave me these two figurines, as a reminder of the possibility of this happening to us." They clearly knew the meaning and clasped each other's forearm with their left hand and pointed their guns with their right hand. In an instant, Cole saw Inola's face in his mind's eye, as they fired simultaneously, their faces contorted and their body's lurched away from each other. Pender arrived on the scene too late, finding them lying next to each other, dead. Shock and disbelief showed on his face, as he bowed his head and prayed for their souls. Pierson, Maggie, Sheriff and the Posse soon gathered around and an ominous silence pervaded. Pender walked slowly down the rocky slope, ignoring Pierson and the Sheriff toward Maggie, with his head down. Maggie began to cry as she embraced him.

Ancient Roman warriors figurines

Pender looked up, tears falling down his face, holding the two figurines in his hand, "They're dead." He broke their embrace, took Maggie's hand in his and walked to their horses, tossing the figurines down to the ground in front of Pierson. They dragged themselves up onto their horses, while the Sheriff looked at them and then back to Pierson in disbelief.

He and the rest of the posse slowly turned and walked to their horses, leaving Pierson standing alone. Pierson knew Cole and Big Black were dead and that Pender and Maggie were leaving. He realized he had lost everything.

Pierson, barely audible, "Please Pen...Pen...Maggie...Maggie," while he slowly walked in their direction, and pleaded, "Please don't leave, don't leave me."

Pender and Maggie slowly rode off. Pierson looked at Sheriff Johnson and the posse, who all ignored him, saddled up and went back to gather the wounded and the dead. Pierson lurched for the last time toward the Sheriff, stumbled and fell to his knees, pathetically crawled on all fours and dug his hands into the earth beneath him. He continued to plead as he groped forward, "Sheriff, please... please don't leave me." Pierson crawled on the ground with his arms out-stretched toward Pender and Maggie as they rode out in one direction, the Sheriff and his posse in another. They left him alone as they disappeared into the distance.

THE END

EPILOGUE

THE BLACK STALLION suddenly appeared, high on the top of a knoll, close to the Cherokee encampment. He reared up on his hind quarters, whinnied and snorted, without a bridle or saddle. Observing the stallion, Inola and Running Horse were joined by some of the braves, trying to make sense as to why the stallion came there, unsaddled, without Cole. The black beauty reared up again, turned and galloped off, out of sight. They all looked at each other, confused and concerned. They had heard there was trouble in town. Inola wanted to ride to the Pierson Ranch immediately to find out what happened, but her father told her not to go. He didn't want her mixed up in any kind of trouble or worse, so he sent two of his braves to find out what had happened.

Inola, very emotional, quickly returned to her lodge, to wait for word. She entered and laid down on her bedding and closed her eyes as she prayed to the Great Spirit for Cole's safety. Inola, hardly able to calm herself, finally drifted into a spiritual slumber.

At dusk, the sky was blue and amber with distant shadows of stars that began to flicker. Inola with her long, shiny black hair flowing, arrived riding bareback. She approached the open field where Cole was waiting atop his horse, and he dismounted as she neared. They were happy to see each other again. Cole greeted Inola with a warm, friendly embrace; not as the child he knew many years ago, but as the beautiful, sensuous woman that she had become. He felt a strong sense of love and excitement being close to her. Inola felt the same, familiar, and yet excited in a new way, to be there with Cole.

Cole led Inola to walk a short way to sit a while. They walked with their arms around each other's waist like friends do, exchanging small talk. As they came to the tall, cool grass, they sat down close to each other. There was an electricity between them that neither could deny. Inola took Cole's face in her hands, gently turned him toward her and looked into his eyes. She softly stroked his face, then touched his lips and kissed him lightly. She pulled away slowly. Cole looked into her eyes, held her close and passionately kissed her. Inola responded as her heart rate quickened and a feeling of lust filled her body.

She carefully removed his belt and lifted her leather dress to expose her thighs. Cole was tender and caring. This was her desire, ever since she saw him on the reservation, bringing the wild horses to her father.

Inola was cuddled in his arms, basked in the afterglow of their passion, as Cole kissed her forehead and her lips. "Coming home, I didn't know what I would find." He paused and then looked into her eyes with a deep expression of sincerity, "I found you." Inola looked at him as a tear of joy moistened her face, "You have taken all of my love." But her dream of desire was not to be, as her spiritual slumber evolved.

The night was dark, very dark. A distant moon was covered by dark grey clouds. The wind whispered an Indian chant, the chant of the dead. A man sat on a horse in the middle of an open field. His arms were out-stretched, facing the dark sky.

He asked the Heavens not to take him, although he knew his time was near. The wind spoke to him as he turned around and it was Cole, seated on his beautiful black stallion, his face and body covered in blood. His eyes were cold and stared straight ahead. He wanted to stay, but knew it was not to be. It was as the wind told him. One moment he was there; the next, he and his horse were gone, swallowed up by a huge grey cloud of dust, followed by a dead silence. Inola had this same vision again, but this time she did not awaken. She saw Cole as he rode away to meet the Great Spirit and to finally be at peace. All the pain he felt, had left him. It was with a deep, heartfelt sadness that Inola knew Cole had left the earth.

Inola sobbed and asked the Great Spirit why, but understood that she must live on. It was not her time. But she believed that at some time in the distance, their spirits joined as one; hers of the black fox and Cole's of the black stallion, would be together again, forever.

Black Stallion

ABOUT THE AUTHOR

MICHAEL DANTE is an Award-Winning Actor and an Award-Winning Author. Michael received the Ella Dickey Literacy Award in 2018 for his autobiography, *Michael Dante-From Hollywood to Michael Dante Way*. He recalls his journey through Hollywood during the Golden Years, leading up to a street named for him in his hometown of Stamford, Connecticut, 'Michael Dante Way.' The 306-page book is full of interesting behind-the-scenes stories and wonderful photographs.

His second book, *Winterhawk's Land*, is the sequel in book form, to the 1976 film in which he played the title role and starred in, Winterhawk. As a noble Blackfoot Chief, he set out to find a cure for smallpox from the white man, who he had never traded with. During the pursuit, Winterhawk and a young missionary girl fall in love. Their lives continued twenty years later, in Winterhawk's Land. He defied the railroad owners and the government from taking 10 miles on either side of the tracks without negotiating, to defend the survival of his People.

Michael Dante has co-starred and appeared in 30 films and 150 television shows and was under contract to three major studios, MGM, 20th Century Fox and Warner Bros. He has received many prestigious film industry and western genre film awards in Hollywood and throughout the country. He played professional baseball before his acting career as a bonus ball player with the Boston Braves and eventually went to spring training with the Washington Senators. His baseball career was cut short by a shoulder injury and Tommy Dorsey, the famous band leader, saw Michael in a play rehearsal at the University of Miami, arranged a screen test for him at MGM Studios, and the rest is history.

www.michaeldanteway.com – imdb.pro
www.facebook.com/groups/MichaelDanteFanClub